ESSENCE OF DESIRE

A Novel with a Mormon Backdrop

By

Niels E. Edlefsen

Publisher
Blue Moon Literary Press
327 Twelfth Street
Davis, CA 95616

www.bluemoonlitartreview.com
530-902-0026
Email: evans327@comcast.net

Dedication

To my wife Carrie for her fifty-six years of love, patience and encouragement, during the vagaries of my career. To my daughters, Ruth and Elaine for their love and with the hope that they and my grandchildren will not be too much embarrassed by my adventure into the literary field.

This re-publication has been inspired by Darwin Garlick Cooper (a great-great grandson of Niels E. Edlefsen).

This story involves the romantic and intellectual activities of some fictional European immigrant converts to Mormonism as that indigenous religion made its turbulent development in America. Courage, confidence, disillusionment, hardship, passion, hope and joy play their roles.

It was raining hard this night in late autumn, 1842, as Borga Borgasen lay in bed in his modest quarters in Nauvoo. But even if the moon had been shining and it had been mid-summer, he could not have slept. His parents were arriving from his native Denmark the following day—arriving with several other immigrants on the *Maid of Iowa* from New Orleans. The river boat was owned and operated by the Mormon Church and would reach Nauvoo, the largest city in Illinois on the east bank of the Mississippi, in the early morning—if it were on time. *The Maid of Iowa* was always on time, Borga thought.

He was thinking right now of his arrival in America and the exciting prospects ahead of him—a whole new world in his grasp. His first stop had been New York. He was an able carpenter and he had found work quickly. A strong, good-looking young man, with large, useful hands, he worked hard and diligently. But his job was not his chief interest. What had commanded his restless spirit, and had brought him to America in the first place, was his interest in religion and the leadership of Joseph Smith, founder of the Mormon Church—or, as many preferred, the Church of Jesus Christ of the Latter-Day Saints. He wanted to be a part of the movement in the new country; he wanted to throw his 6-foot-two, 190 pounds into the Mormon growth and development with all the vigor his youth and ambitions allowed.

Now Borga lay in bed, wondering. His experiences had not quite worked out as he had expected. There had been violence, even bloodshed. There had been rumors of a price on Joseph Smith's head. He personally had been involved in some of the violence. He certainly agreed with the basic principles of the church, but his interpretation of some points had been seriously questioned by fellow Mormons. Could he explain his new philosophy to his deeply religious father and his gentle mother on the morrow, when the *Maid of Iowa* docked a Nauvoo? Would they understand his changed attitude since leaving Denmark at the age of nineteen?

He had written such glowing reports home, avoiding the disturbing things that had confronted him, and withholding practically all the information about the violence with which the church had been involved.

He had been such an apt student of the Bible while growing up in Denmark and had been encouraged wisely by his parents, and especially his grandfather. But even as a lad of seventeen he had begun to ask questions of his Lutheran minister, and the answers to some questions were not to his liking. For example, why had the minister the authority to speak as a man of God? His parents, it seemed, never questioned anything. His parents, he knew, would never understand; they would wonder about a son of theirs who had doubts in his mind.

The next morning, after a sleepless night, Borga was among the first to reach the water's edge as the *Maid of Iowa* came into sight; and as the river boat neared the bank he could already see his father's six-foot-two frame, with his long, black beard—and his blond mother Christine, much shorter, standing beside her husband. Then he spotted his sister Hedvig, blonde like her mother, and so changed from the last time he saw her.

They were the first off the river boat, and everyone was talking at once as they greeted their son and brother. Standing slightly to the rear was a Welsh family with whom they had become acquainted on the journey from New Orleans—a Mr. and Mrs. Evans and their seventeen-year-old daughter Ethel. Borga smiled. He noted her dark red hair and her well-shaped body and had it been any other time than right now he might have had an emotional response. But now his parents and sister were in America, and all his thought were taken up in welcoming them. Borga and his father had so much to talk about, so they spent most of the day in the son's modest quarters while the mother and the Welsh family explored the town.

"You won't have any trouble getting work, father," Borga told his male parent. "There's a great need in America for skilled carpenters."

"If I were only young like you are," the father said. "Every-thing is so new, so promising, in this country." The old man sighed. "Tell me more."

"Well, I met your old army friend Jens Pedersen, like you suggested," Borga went on, "and he is quite interested in this Mormon religion. He and a Captain Peter Dahl, who operates the *Carl Jacobsen*, are very active in moving immigrants from Sweden and Denmark by river into the Minnesota territory. These are mostly farmers looking for rich, virgin land. I think we should follow them. There'll be a lot of carpenter work to do."

"I am interested in good land and work, but first I have some questions."

"What, father?"

"What about this new church?"

"What about it?" Borga knew the questions he didn't want to answer were coming.

"Do you attend the church?" his father asked.

"Oh, yes," Borga said, and swallowed hard. "I was much im-pressed. I was much impressed by Joseph Smith on the several occasions I attended meetings. He speaks with eloquence and emotion and in no time has his audience following his every word. He seems a very competent leader."

"If it is not out of order, I must attend some of these meetings," the father said, smiling at his tall son.

"Really, the immigrants are following the new movement west," Borga said. "It is growing and growing and..." He left the sentence hanging.

"You didn't finish, son," the father prompted.

"The Prophet—that is, Brother Smith—has visions and I can't believe—" He stopped again and put his arm about his father's shoulders. "Father, it's getting late and I think we should go and find the others." He did not have the courage to tell his father of his doubts, or to lay out in detail some of the violence he had witnessed.

2

Even before his parents' arrival in America, Borga had become quite involved in the Mormon movement notwithstanding some of his doubts. He went to church regularly although he had not become a member. It was during this period that Brigham Young, a former Methodist, became active in the movement.

Borga took every opportunity to get information about the leaders of the Church, and their thinking about each other and their personalities.

New people were moving into the city at a high rate. There were many non-believers among them, some very hostile, and Borga wanted to get all the information that he could, so he spoke with believers as well as non-believers.

One non-Mormon, who said that he knew Joseph Smith as a young man, told Borga that "Joseph had little ambition and some vey laudable aspirations; his mother's intellect showed out of him feebly, especially when he used to help us solve some questions of moral or physical ethics in our juvenile debating club."

Borga spent some time at the print shop, where a printer who had known Joseph told him "he was known among the young men I associated with as a romancer of the first water. I never knew so ignorant a man as Joe to have so fertile an imagination. He could never tell of a common occurrence in his daily life without embellishing the story with his imagination."

A former Methodist minister who had joined the Mormon Church and had become disgruntled and apostatized published a letter in which he stated, "Have you not frequently observed in Joseph a want of that sobriety, prudence and stability which are some of the most prominent traits in a Christian character? Have you not often discovered in him a spirit of lightness and levity, a temper easily irritated, and habitual proneness to jesting and joking? Some suppose his weakness, nay his wickedness, can form no reasonable objection to his revelations."

Joseph Smith had become angered at something that Sidney Rigdon, his close associate, had done, although it was not clear to Borga what the difficulty was all about. In one sermon Joseph Smith said, "And now behold, verily I say unto you, I, the Lord, am not pleased with my servant Sidney Rigdon. He exalted himself in his heart and received not counsel but grieved the spirit;" and at another point, "I can contend with wicked men and devils—yes, with angels. No power can pluck these keys from me, except the power that gave them to me; that was Peter, James and John, but for what Sidney had done the devil shall handle him as one man handles another."

Borga learned that Sidney Rigdon was not at the meeting but that when it was reported to him, he commented, "Is it possible that I have been deceived? But if Joseph says so, it is so."

At one meeting where Brigham Young was preaching, he stated, "When I first undertook to sound the doctrine of Mormonism, I supposed I could handle it as I could the Methodists, Presbyterians, or other creeds of Christendom, which I had paid considerable attention to. I found all religions so deficient in doctrine that when I tried to tie loose ends or fragments together, they would break in my hands.

"When I commenced to examine Mormonism, I found it impossible to take hold of either end of it. I found it was from eternity, passing through time and into eternity again. When I discovered this, I said, 'It is worthy of notice of men,' then applied my heart to wisdom and sought diligently for understanding."

Borga was impressed by the difference in these three leaders. Joseph Smith was tall, handsome, jovial, imaginative and had a ready sense of humor, with an outgoing personality. Sidney Rigdon had been a Baptist minister and was very solemn. He was well-educated with little sense of humor and a tendency to emotional irritability at times. Brigham Young, a former Methodist and Mason, was sturdy, wise, loyal and generally moderate in manner, with a mild sense of humor.

Jens Pedersen, Borga's close friend, and Borga, finally joined the Church and were baptized by immersion, as in the original Christian church.

3

In response to the Church leaders emphasizing the need for missionary work, Borga was invited to accompany Caleb Jones on a journey. "This will be good experience for you, Borga."

"I do not believe that I know the principles of the Church well enough to speak. Also, I lack the emotional zeal which you exhibit."

"I know, Borga, from the questions you have raised that you have studied the *Book of Mormon* thoroughly. I will introduce you as a new investigator, then you tell about some of the interesting information that you have acquired from your studies."

Borga was a little apprehensive, but finally agreed to accompany Caleb. They arrived at their destination early in the evening and decided to hold their meeting on the main street corner in town. The singing of a hymn started the curious in town moving in that direction. Following the hymn, Caleb offered a prayer. By the time he was through praying a crowd had assembled.

Caleb introduced Borga. "We have with us tonight a young investigator who has left the shores of Europe to seek religious freedom which this great country of ours guarantees. Brother Borgasen has carefully studied the information which the *Book of Mormon* furnishes us regarding the American Indians. I have asked him to outline for us some of what he has learned about that subject. Brother Borgasen."

Borga noticed some mumblings in the group when the *Book of Mormon* was announced. "I will report briefly," he said "on what I have learned about the American Indians from my studies of the *Book of Mormon*. This Book is a translation by Joseph Smith of writings on *Golden Plates*. The *Plates* were bound by three large rings and were left by the last of the ancient Nephite people during the War of Destruction, about the year 421 A.D. They were buried in the Hill of Cumorah in New York State. Joseph Smith was directed, by an angel of the Lord, to where they were located.

"A small group of people came from Babylon to the Americas about 2200 B.C. Another small group came from Palestine to the Americas about 600 B.B. Also, another small group came from Jerusalem to the Americas about 590 B.B. These groups settled in various parts of the south, central and north America.

"The Americas were anciently inhabited by these people forming four great civilizations: the Jaradites, the Nephites, the Lamanites, and the Mulekites.

"The Jaradites, the first nation, destroyed themselves long before the other three nations developed, but they left their records. The Nephite, Lamanite and Mulekite nations destroyed each other, ending in the eastern part of North America where they had compiled their history while engraving it in their language of hieroglyphics on the *Golden Plates*.

"A few of the dark-skinned Lamanites survived. Many of the American Indians are of these people."

As soon as Borga finished his speech, Caleb stood up and started to relate how Joseph Smith had received a revelation and how God had spoken to him. The crowd had increased in size and had become rather noisy. He was forced, by interruptions from individuals in the group, to respond to questions. One man shouted, "We don't need to learn about your Prophet, we have one of our own." This was followed by loud laughter. "I am sorry, sir," said Caleb, "there are many false prophets."

A woman responded, "My son ain't no false prophet." She indicated that the puny looking young man in his teens standing next to her was her son. "God revealed his will to my son, and he is organizing the true Christian church on this earth."

"Now what do you think of that?" shouted one in the crowd.

Caleb responded, "My good woman, your son has been subjected to the buffets of Satan. You should humble yourself in prayer and seek God's forgiveness."

"Her son is just as much a prophet as your Mormon prophet, Joseph Smith."

"You'd better go home. We don't need you," shouted another in the crowd in a loud voice. Another shouted, "Let's get rid of these Mormon bastards!"

Caleb responded, "In this country we have a right to discuss any religion we wish."

"Oh, is that so? We'll see about that," shouted one man. He turned to some of his followers. "Some of you men go get these Mormons, and some of the rest of you get some tar and feathers."

Six men rushed up and grabbed Caleb and Borga. "Rip the clothes of the bastards, and throw them to the ground, spread eagle so we can give them a nice coast of tar," shouted one.

"It is too bad we have to put you on cold, frozen ground before we give you a nice coat of warm feathers," grinned another.

Caleb and Borga tried to reason with the men but to no avail. There was too much liquor, and there were too many men. They were all shouting and cursing.

When the men returned with the tar, they fiendishly covered the victims' bodies with it, rubbing it well into all their hair. One man shouted, "Now, we'll give you a nice warm coat of feathers. Then you can go home because we won't need you anymore."

It was late at night and quite cold when the crowd dispersed leaving the two missionaries to make their way home as best they could. They gathered up what they could find of their clothes and made their way to the Gilbert and Whitney store.

Mr. Gilbert furnished them with some oil which mixed with the tar enabled them to remove most of it, after which they finished the job with warm water and soap.

When they were all cleaned up Caleb was aware that Borga was very much depressed over the experience. "Borga, you must not let this discourage you. God is testing our faith and sincerity."

"I did not realize that intelligent people could behave so violently," said Borga.

4

Early in the Mormon movement, Joseph Smith conceived of the Church as a gathering of Israel. He dispatched missionaries to the sparsely settled area of the Indian territory in Missouri. They made an enthusiastic report about the possibilities of settlement there.

As a result, he immediately decided on a course of action. The church would establish the Order of Enoch, a new Jerusalem, the City of the Saints. He led a group of elders to Independence, Missouri, and established a colony by moving one entire congregation to the new location.

The Order of Enoch was a somewhat communistic movement. Each member settling in Missouri consecrated all his goods to the Church. All was deposited in the Bishop's storehouse. The Bishop was to purchase land and to settle the members on it. Each member could draw on the storehouse according to his needs.

But the Mormon attitude toward slavery, the socialistic economy of the Mormons, secret rituals practiced in the Mormon temple, and the Mormon theology all combined to make for hostility among the Missourians. They forced the Mormons to leave Independence, Jackson County. News of the expulsion of the Mormons was sent back to Joseph Smith at his headquarters. This changed his advice to the Mormons from "be wise as serpents and harmless as doves" attitude to a more hostile one.

Stories had been flying thick and fast that some important announcement was to be made in church on Sunday morning. A sudden hush came over the audience as Joseph Smith arose to speak. He opened by telling the audience what the Mormons were experiencing at the hands of Missourians and ended in great anger by stating, "Behold, I say unto you, that the redemption of Zion must needs come by power. Therefore, I will rise up unto my people, a man who shall lead them like Moses led the people of Israel; for ye are the children of Israel and the seed of Abraham, and we must needs be led out of bondage, by power with the outstretched arm."

Following his angry outburst in church, Joseph Smith organized an army of two hundred men, which he called *The Zion's Camp* to go to the aid of the Saints in Missouri. Caleb Jones, Jens Pedersen and Borga were among the first to be "called." Borga's sense of loyalty was becoming strong. He felt that it was his duty to go to the aid of the Saints, who, from his observations, were trying to carry out the principles of the Gospel as taught by Joseph Smith. Borga noted that many undesirable things were happening, both by members of the Church, as well as by non-members. He felt, however, that they were the result of human weaknesses rather than the result of any of the Prophet's teachings.

The Prophet appointed Lyman Wight as general. He had served in the War of 1812. Brigham Young was appointed as one of the captains. Borga, and several others, were assigned to Brigham Young's unit. Joseph Smith was with the organization and, of course, General Wight reported to him.

Borga wanted to know, "Is this activity the result of a commandment of God?"

"It is," assured Caleb Jones.

"Then we must support it."

The news that the Church was sending an army to restore Zion was a source of great rejoicing to the Saints in Missouri, but it stimulated great hostility among the Gentiles. A messenger carried the news back to Smith that in a new attack over two hundred houses had been burned.

"How many are there in the mobs?" inquired Joseph.

"There are probably hundreds, and additional hundreds if the State Troopers are included."

As the march progressed, tension and dissatisfaction built up. "Why," cried one man, "should I risk my life for the people of Missouri?"

"Because God has commanded it," answered Caleb Jones.

"How do I know that it is God's will that I should desert my wife and children and get murdered?"

"I think you are losing your faith. You had better go and humble yourself in prayer," urged Caleb.

With inadequate food and badly overburdened animals, they moved day after day through the heat and the dust over one thousand miles of poor roads.

The cursing, limping, sweating and footsore men pushed on with enemies all about them. Sharpshooters had come from Missouri to intercept them; there were Indians and wild animals; and, worst of all, was the blasphemy, illness and death in their midst.

An epidemic of cholera spread through *Zion's Camp* taking the lives of several and incapacitating many. Borga was ill at the time when the Prophet announced a revelation that "All victory and glory are brought to pass through your diligence, faithfulness and prayers." Joseph explained that the Lord was trying the faith of his flock.

Word was received at *Zion's Camp* that when the Mormons were driven out of Independence, Missouri, an agreement with the Missourian authorities was reached that the Saints would be allowed to move across the Missouri River and settle further north. Some settled in DeWitt, Clay County, while others located in Caldwell County. Still further north in Davies County a colony was established at Adam-ondi-Ahman.

Conditions under which the men of *Zion's Camp* had to march were not only bad but considerable bickering between the men took place during the march and few had had any army experience. The food was poor and many of the men were emotionally not conditioned for such an ordeal. Borga was surprised to find so much instability. Some imagined spies were in their ranks, others talked of rumors that angels were flying over their heads.

They were urged to keep the identity of Joseph Smith secret for as long as they could. They tried not to let it be known that they were Mormons. Hostility was evidenced in areas along their path by the Gentiles, and especially when they reached the troubled area near Independence. These things caused Joseph to change his mind. The warlike attitude was dropped as futile. In spite of this, the Prophet did not give up the idea of the *redemption of Zion in Missouri*. But as the *Zion's Camp* approached Jackson County, Missouri, it became clear that the Jackson County cause had been lost. The government and the Gentiles were too strong and hostile.

Joseph had a revelation. He announced that the situation was not yet suitable for "the redemption of Zion in Jackson County." He consulted with attorneys who confirmed his feeling that the Mormons had legal rights in their favor.

Joseph ceased all hostile attitudes and set about cultivating a feeling of good will between the Saints and their neighbors in Clay County. He felt that he had done all he could, so decided to abandon *Zion's Camp*.

5

Trouble soon broke out. About one month later, on election day, a group of Saints, unarmed, turned up to vote. They were met by a group of rowdy, hostile Missourians, some of them drunk. They were itching for a fight. One of the men shouted, "What do you damn Mormons want?" The Mormon leader said, "We only wish to cast our vote."

"Oh," shouted the rowdy, "did you boys hear that? These damned Mormons think they're going to vote."

Another one called out, "We don't let Mormons vote no more than negroes."

A large, rough-looking character pushed to the front. "If any of you want to try something, let your best man come forward and I'll show you the way we handle Mormons in Missouri."

"We don't want trouble, but we intend to vote," announced Borga.

"Oh, no, you won't!" the man screamed, as he lunged forward and landed a blow to Borga's face. The fight was on and was bloody, but there were too many Mormons and the Missourians retreated; but they vowed to get the Mormons later.

The Saints returned to their homes, gathered their families and went into hiding. One went as a messenger to Joseph Smith to ask for help.

Following the fight on election day, Governor Boggs instructed the Mormons they had no alternative but to leave the state.

As preparations were being made to carry out the order, one group was camping at a place called Shoals Creek. While they were deciding on their next move, a group of Missourians rode up and one of the representatives asked, "Are you people Mormons?"

"Yes, we are," answered Borga.

"You must leave immediately," ordered the Missourians.

"But why?" protested Borga. "We are law-abiding Americans and have given no cause for offense."

"You are Mormons. That is offense enough!" the spokesman added. "Within ten days every Mormon must be out of Missouri or men, women and children will be shot down indiscriminately. No mercy will be shown. It is the order of the governor that you shall be exterminated. And, by God, you will be!"

Later in the afternoon, the men and women of the Mormon group went about their duties and the children were playing, when suddenly some of them noticed that a group of men was riding toward their camp. Borga went out to attempt to make peace, since he observed that they were probably Missouri militiamen. The Missourians, about two hundred strong, obviously stimulated by liquor, paid no attention to him, and at that point the Mormons in the camp began to flee for safety. The militiamen opened fire. Every effort was made to get the children, and all those who were able to move, into the woods and to buildings nearby. The women quickly dashed to help get the children protected from the fire.

Borga dropped to a position near a ravine. A bullet passed through his shirt, grazing his right side. He dropped down behind the ridge so that they no longer could see him, and then crept down the ravine under the ridge of earth where he felt protected from the bullets. He had used all his ammunition and had killed two Missourians. He was horrified as he saw one of the young boys attacked. His head was literally blown in half when a rifle was put close to his head. Borga heard one of the attackers nearby say, "That was a damned shame to kill that little boy." The other one said, "Damn the difference! Nits grow up to be lice."

As the Missourians, who had just killed the young boy, came walking by, Borga jumped out from behind the bushes under which he was hiding and felled the Missourian with a blow to his head with the butt of his gun. As the shooting ceased Borga heard the leader call out, "Let's get the hell out of here!"

Borga then rushed to the log building nearby thinking of two teenage boys whom he had seen flee there at the time the shooting began. All was quiet within the building. He stepped inside and stood aghast to find that both the children had been killed along with the others.

One little girl must have tried to run for the woods but did not make it. One arm was almost shot away and the main artery was punctured by the bullet, causing massive bleeding.

Borga was appalled when he realized that he was apparently the only one left to take care of the others. It was an overpowering situation. He tried hard to keep his senses in order to help save as many lives as he could. Moans and cries were coming from all directions, and darkness was rapidly approaching. How could he possibly take care of so many people who needed immediate attention? There were no bandages, no drugs or medical facilities nearby.

Sizing up the terrible situation he quickly proceeded to take care of the minor injuries of those who looked as if they could survive. What a relief when he spotted several women, one only slightly wounded and others who had escaped injury entirely, coming out of the woods.

They banded together and used all their capabilities and imagination to relieve the suffering of their brothers and sisters. Groaning and crying could be heard throughout the night. They were terrified and their hearts were broken when they realized that only two men had escaped the hands of the murderers.

6

Borga rode back immediately to Far West to inform the authorities of the slaughter at Haun's Mill. When he got there, he found that several other riders had brought reports of other similar attacks. Another rider brought word that Generals Lucas and Doniphan were marching on Far West with a large group of men. Still another rider brought a report that a large force of Missourians, dressed as Indians and covered with war paint, were joining up with General Lucas and his militiamen.

Joseph Smith hurriedly consulted with some of his advisors, among them being Lyman Wight, who was the general in charge of the *Zion Camp*, Parley Pratt and Sidney Rigdon. After a brief conference with these three fiery brethren, Joseph told them that he must seek advice from God and retired to prayer. After he had gone, Wight shouted, "Now, by God, we've got to fight."

"You're damn right we got to fight. What do you think is our first move?" asked Pratt.

"If we marched away from here," said Wight, "they would kill and rape our wives and children. We must fortify Far West and make them take us by an attack."

Pratt in anguish exclaimed, "I wish Joseph would return so we could consult with him."

"Oh, to hell with that," said Wight. "It is too late for prayers now. Three thousand men will probably attack us tomorrow. You round up the guns and ammunition. I will get the men and women and children busy building fortifications."

Joseph had not only prayed, he had sent word to another Mormon at De Witt, Colonel Hinkle, of the Mormon Legion, to take his men and contact General Lucas and try to see if the difficulties could be worked out peaceably.

Joseph arrived back in Far West early in the evening to find everyone working feverishly in preparation for the battle which they anticipated in the morning.

Shortly after Joseph's arrival, Colonel Hinkle came riding towards Far West. Wight looked with disdain. "I wouldn't trust that bastard as far as I can throw a bull by the tail."

Hinkle announced, "General Lucas will meet with you, Joseph, and your advisors under a flag of truce."

After some discussion in which Hinkle was noncommittal, Joseph Smith, Sidney Rigdon, Clarence Smith, Lyman Wight, and Parley Pratt rode out to meet General Lucas. When they arrived, they were shown an agreement which Colonel Hinkle had signed. It called for all the Mormon ammunition and guns to be forfeited, the leaders to surrender and stand trial for treason. All property was to be confiscated. All the Mormons to agree peacefully to leave Missouri.

Joseph was aghast and argued with Lucas, to no avail, that Hinkle had no authority to sign such an agreement.

All the Mormons in the group, except Hinkle, were imprisoned. During the night they were subjected to a tirade of mockery, obscenities, blasphemy and abuse. One guard called out, "Come on, Joseph Smith, show us an angel." Another said, "Give us one of your revelations."

In court the next morning the charges were reviewed, and they were found guilty and sentenced to death. General Doniphan was told, "Sir, you will take Joseph Smith and the other prisoners into the public square at 9:00 o'clock tomorrow morning and shoot them."

General Doniphan replied, "It is coldblooded murder. I will not obey your orders. My brigade shall march for liberty tomorrow morning at 8:00 o'clock. If you execute these men, I will hold you responsible before an early tribunal, so help me God!"

The Mormons left at camp were uninformed as to what had happened to their leaders under General Clark, representing the governor. In the afternoon, all the residents were ordered into the public square, which he surrounded with his troops.

Sitting on his horse he announced, "I am General Clark. Colonel Hinkle, your military leader, agreed to four terms to save you from destruction. The first was that you surrender your leaders and this you have done. The second was that you give up your arms. The third was that you sign your property over to pay for the cost of this war."

He remained quiet for a few seconds to let the result of his comments sink in. "Another article yet remains for you to comply with, and that is that you leave the state forthwith, and whatever may be your feelings concerning this, or whatever your innocence, it is nothing to me.

"I am here to see that the terms of the treaty are fulfilled. The character of this state has suffered almost beyond redemption from the character, conduct and influence that you have exerted, and we deem it an act of justice to restore her character to its original standing among the states by every proper means."

He hesitated for a moment, and there was complete silence among the more than one thousand people listening to him.

"The orders of the governor to me were that you should be exterminated and not allowed to remain in the state, and had your leaders not complied with the terms of the treaty before this, you and your families would have been destroyed and your homes would be in ashes. You must not think of staying here another season or of putting in crops, for the moment you do this the citizens will be upon you."

Knowing that Caleb Jones had been included in the fifty men arrested, Borga rushed toward Caleb's home to see if he could help Mrs. Jones and her children.

He had no sooner started than he heard loud yells and galloping horses. Looking around he saw a large group of men painted up as Indians, well-armed and apparently well-supplied with liquor, dashing among the people. Borga was held up in his efforts to reach Caleb's home by the terrific confusion and disturbance following the arrival of these men. They cursed and pushed people around and took a fiendish delight in shooting cattle and horses.

When Borga finally got to Caleb's home, he saw through the open door three men. They had stripped the clothing off Mrs. Jones, and two of them were holding her on the bed while the third was attacking her. Borga grabbed a club and dashed into the room delivering blows to the back of the man attacking her.

He was grabbed immediately and beaten into unconsciousness. He partially regained his senses long enough to attempt to get up but was knocked down again and whipped brutally by the men until he again lost consciousness.

When he came to, he found himself in a strange home with Jens standing by. Some of the people had moved him to this place and Jens, with their help, had partially tended his wounds.

7

During the months of imprisonment in Missouri for Joseph Smith, and other Mormons, the exodus of the Mormons began, and Brigham Young led the flock "into the wilderness." He selected several men including Borga, Caleb and Jens as scouts to find suitable land in Illinois and Iowa on which the Mormons could settle. Through underground communications Joseph Smith and the other prisoners learned of the exodus, were successful in bribing guards, and managed to escape to join the moving band.

As soon as Joseph was free, he moved vigorously to obtain land on the west and east side of the Mississippi River, in Iowa and Illinois. He dealt with a government land agent. The Mormons had no money when they left Missouri and precious little other than what they could bring in their wagons. However, they did bring the deeds to their property in Missouri and Joseph traded these deeds to obtain the new property.

This period gave Joseph an opportunity to let his imagination dwell upon theological matters. He pondered on the behavior of the religious leaders of old, as recorded in the Bible. He was impressed by their many references to the wives that the prophets and leaders had.

He conceived of the intriguing possibility of inter-weaving the ideas of plural marriage into his ideas of man's progressions from the pre-earthly existence through the early experience and into the celestial kingdom. The more he thought about it the more he was convinced that it was the will of God.

Joseph cautiously approached his leaders, one at a time, with a pledge of secrecy and convinced them that it was the will of God. It was not easy, but Joseph was persistent, even though there was considerable fear expressed that there would be serious repercussions from the Gentiles, as well as from some members of the church. At first only a few of the leaders were to participate in the practice of plural marriage.

Caleb Jones was one of the favored brethren. He had a wife, Clara, and two children. He decided to discuss the matter confidentially with Borga, his young, unmarried friend and confidante.

"What on earth are you talking about, Caleb?"

"I am telling you the truth as revealed through the Prophet."

"It does not sound like the word of God to me. I think it is horrifying."

"The Prophet has assured us that it is the word of God."

"I can't believe that such a thing is true," protested Borga.

"It seems clear," urged Caleb, "that the more wives a man has in this life, the more exalted will be his position in the celestial kingdom."

"Does Clara know about this? What does she think about it?"

"I haven't discussed it with her."

"It sounds like the dream of a mad man, Caleb."

"It's the Lord's commandment, Borga, and I suggest that you ask Him yourself, in humble prayer, as I have done."

Borga was yielding. He said, "Well," as he struggled with his feelings, "I can't believe it."

"I am certain that you will," continued Caleb. "Go ask God for understanding."

"I will. Only He alone can convince me that this is a commandment."

Taking Borga by the arm Caleb said, "Go pray, Borga, and then we shall talk further."

Caleb Jones was anxious to put the principles into practice. He went walking by the creek where he had seen Jenny Storm strolling several times. She was about eighteen, he thought, and she seemed an intelligent, strong girl. He had heard that she was very thoughtful, and incredibly determined at times. "Good morning, Sister Jenny. It's a beautiful day after the rain."

"Yes, it is. The flowers and foliage seem so clean and beautiful."

"Jenny, I have something I want to discuss with you. Let us sit down here and talk." She was surprised and apprehensive. "I have known you for some time and I want you to be my wife."

Jenny leaped to her feet. "You are out of your mind!" she cried.

"It is God's will, Sister Jenny. Come and sit down." He pulled her down beside him. "You'll feel the punishment of God if you resist His will. The Prophet has announced that it is to be."

"You are already married," she protested.

"Yes, but I must prepare for the next world. It would not be sinful, Jenny dear. The Prophet would not allow women to be led into sin."

"It seems like sin to me."

He pulled her to him and kissed her on the cheek. She was annoyed because she did not mind it. "You must consent to be my wife, Sister Jenny."

"Absolutely not," she protested.

"Do not resist. This is an opportunity to be exalted in heaven. Only certain of the leaders of the Church have been authorized by the Prophet to take plural wives."

"Well!" She started to say something and had a troubled expression on her face. "If the Prophet has sanctioned it, it must not be sinful." Caleb was quite a fine man, she thought. "I must go home now, Brother Caleb. I'll think about it."

"You must keep it a secret."

"I probably can't," she said.

8

Borga, up to this point, had never questioned anything which Joseph Smith had revealed as the word of God, but this whole question of plural marriage was getting the church into serious trouble. He was beginning to have some doubts. His father was rapidly becoming very devout and chided his son. "Borga, you seem to be losing your faith. If the Prophet reveals it, how dare you question it?"

Borga decided not to disturb the faith which his father had developed.

The enemies of the church were becoming active again. The city charter gave almost complete control of all affairs to the city of Nauvoo. A legion of 4,000 men had been organized, with Lieutenant General Joseph Smith as commanding officer. When fears of attack on the Mormons by their enemies was discussed with Joseph, he tended to put great reliance in his legion. Some of the church's more practical followers, however, felt that the only way to combat the kind of enemies with which they were faced was on a man-to-man basis. The river was handy for easy disposal for those of the enemy who became too troublesome.

As the city prospered and became the largest city in Illinois, and the Temple was nearly completed, the antagonism to the Mormons increased. Some apostates were especially active.

Some extremely critical articles were published in the *Nauvoo Expositor*. These stirred up Joseph's anger, especially since they were attacks in his own territory.

A city council meeting was held at which Joseph ordered the sheriff to destroy the *Expositor* press. The job was done, and nothing could have been more effective in irritating the enemies of the Church. The territories surrounding Nauvoo became seething with antagonistic citizens.

A committee from Carthage, the county seat, met with Governor Ford. He was urged to call out the state militia. He delayed action. The owners of the *Expositor* had issued warrants for the arrest of Joseph Smith and the councilmen. But Joseph, under the city charter, had invoked the power of habeas corpus. Governor Ford issued orders for the Mormon representatives to come to Carthage and present their case. He was well aware that the destruction of the *Expositor* press was a serious crime in the United States, where there was strong feeling regarding the freedom of the press.

Governor Ford sent word to Nauvoo that if the Mormon leaders would come to Carthage, he would send a party to protect them. There was some disagreement among the Mormons as to whether they should rely on such a promise. It was finally decided to provide a party of their own to accompany the leaders to Carthage.

Two charges were placed against Joseph—inciting to riot because of the *Expositor* incident, and treason, because it was felt that he intended to set up a kingdom of his own in Nauvoo. A hearing was held at which he and his aides were bound over by the court on the first charge; the second charge was not discussed. He went back to his room in the hotel, however, and there they were arrested for treason and placed in confinement without hearing, on the second floor of a building near the jail. The room contained a bed and some furniture consisting of chairs and a cabinet.

Before departing for Nauvoo to investigate the charges, Governor Ford visited with Joseph. He stated that he agreed with Joseph on all points, except that of the destruction of the press. "The press of the United States," he said, "is looked upon as the great bulwark of American freedom."

"Could we," Joseph asked, "suffer a set of worthless vagabonds to come into our city, and right under our own eyes and protection, vilify and culminate not only ourselves but the characters of our wives and daughters, as was impudently and unblushingly done in that infamous, filthy sheet? There is not a city in the United States that would have suffered such an indignity for twenty-four hours."

Joseph was concerned for his life, and asked permission from Governor Ford to accompany him back to Nauvoo.

One of Joseph's aides had investigated a disturbance outside the jail during the night and had been told by a guard, "We have had too much trouble to get old Joe here to let him ever escape alive, and unless you want to die with him you had better leave before sundown."

But when told of this the governor replied, "You are unnecessarily alarmed for your friends, sir. People are not that cruel."

While waiting for the governor to return, serious discussion took place among the imprisoned Mormons.

"Brother Joseph," confided Willard Richards, "if it is necessary that you die in this manner and if they will take me for your stead, I will suffer for you."

Being of a more violent temperament, John Taylor said, "Brother Joseph, if you will permit it, and say the word, I will have you out of this prison in five hours—if the jail has to come down to do it."

Taylor's plan was to go back to Nauvoo and get the Mormon legion. The gentle Hiram Smith asked them to sing, but Taylor answered, "Brother, I do not feel like singing."

If you commence singing," urged Hiram, "you will get the spirit of it."

John Taylor walked to the window. Surrounding Carthage was a large group of men with their faces painted black and all were armed. There were many more of them than there were guards in the militia. The militiamen meekly submitted to the mob and were marched away. Other members of the mob forced the jail door, rushed upstairs, and fired several shots through the locked door of the room containing the prisoners.

One bullet killed Hiram Smith. Joseph had retained a revolver. He rushed to the door and fired three shots into the crowd in the stairway, while Taylor fended off some of the revolvers now being fired through the partly opened door.

As the door yielded Taylor ran for the window and was shot in the leg from behind, while another bullet hit him in the chest as he reached the window, causing him to fall backward. Joseph tried to leap from the window but was hit by bullets from within the room as well as from outside. Just before his body tumbled to the ground he cried out, "Oh Lord, my God!"

Willard Richards, a calm man, was with the Prophet in Carthage, but was not killed. The governor asked him to pledge his honor to try to keep the Mormons calm.

The next day the bodies were placed on a wagon and returned to Nauvoo. The entire city turned out to meet the procession—most in tears as it passed. The bodies lay in state while an estimated 25,000 Mormons passed to see the features of their leader for the last time. At the burial, large groups of people watched the coffins being lowered. They were unaware that the bodies were not in the boxes. A few leaders had removed the bodies during the night and had made a secret burial. They were afraid of what the enemy might do with the bodies of the dead leaders.

There was grave talk concerning the probable new leader. Caleb Jones, Borga, his father, and Jens Pedersen met frequently for informal discussions. Their talk centered about the current topic.

"What is going to happen?" Borga inquired of Caleb. "Several of the Twelve Apostles are in England, and the others are on missions in distant parts of the United States."

"Yes, this catastrophe has occurred at a very bad time for the Church," Caleb said.

"Which Apostles," inquired Jens Pedersen, "are in the East now?"

Borga volunteered, "Brigham Young and Orson Pratt are in Europe; Wilford Woodruff and Heber Kimball are in New England, while Sidney Rigdon is in Pennsylvania. Parley Pratt and George A. Smith are also on Eastern missions. Willard Richards and John Taylor, who was wounded, are in Nauvoo."

"They have all been requested to return to Nauvoo," announced Caleb. "Some are expected any time now."

Borga's father wanted to know of Caleb. "Who has the final approval of the president?"

"No matter who is considered, the Twelve Apostles have the final vote," answered Caleb.

The next day, the petulant, first assistant to the Prophet, Sidney Rigdon, arrived from Pennsylvania with a revelation, he claimed, in which God had commanded him to be guardian of the Church. He did not wait for the other leaders to return, but immediately called for a meeting of the Mormon community.

He arose and solemnly began. "Gentlemen, you are used up. Gentlemen, you are divided. The anti-Mormons have got you. The brethren are voting every way—some for James, some for Deming, some for Carlson, some for Biddle. The anti-Mormons have got you. You can't stay in the country. Everything is in confusion; you can do nothing. You lack a great leader. You want a head, and unless you unite upon that head, you are blown to the four winds. The anti-Mormons will carry the election. A guardian must be appointed!"

He could not have done better if he had desired to antagonize the Mormons. George A. Smith, in the audience, arose to reply, "Brethren, Elder Rigdon is entirely mistaken. There is no division. The brethren are united. The election will be unanimous, and the friends of law and order will be elected by a thousand majority. There is no occasion to be alarmed. Brother Rigdon is inspiring fears, for which there are no grounds."

A date of August 8 was set at which a decision was to be made. By hard travelling, all the Apostles arrived in time for the morning meeting on the 8th. Sidney Rigdon made his speech to the leaders, closing it by saying, "I have discharged my duty and done what God commanded me, and the people can please themselves whether they accept me or not."

In the morning, during a two-hour speech, Rigdon tried strenuously to convince them that his revelation was a commandment of God.

Brigham Young, president of the Twelve Apostles, arose to reply, "I do not care who leads the church." He said, "But one thing I must know and that is what God says about it. I have the keys and the means of obtaining the mind of God on the subject." Further on, he stated, "Joseph conferred upon our heads all the keys and the powers belonging to the apostleship which he himself held before he was taken away, and no man or set of men can get between Joseph and the Twelve in this world, or in the world to come."

At the end of his speech the meeting was adjourned until 2:00 P.M.

The afternoon general meeting, open for all the Saints, was held in a meadow below the Temple and overlooking the Mississippi River. No meeting house was large enough to hold them.

The enormous audience assembled for the afternoon session and Brigham Young arose. "Attention all!" A sudden hush went over the audience; most did not know that he had returned.

As president of the Twelve Apostles he made his report, during which he stated, "For the first time in my life, for the first time in your lives, for the first time in the Kingdom of God, in the nineteenth century, without a Prophet at our head, do I step forth to act in my calling in connection with the Quorum of the Twelve, as apostles of Jesus Christ unto this generation."

He presented the recommendation of the Twelve Apostles to the general membership for their consideration. He asked for a show of hands as to whether they approved or not.

The vote was almost unanimous, and Brigham Young became the new president of the Mormon Church.

9

Shortly after Brigham Young was made president, Caleb Jones and the emigrants from Denmark held one of their many formal meetings. Caleb opened with the comment, "It seems a curious thing that the leader of the original Christian church was persecuted and became a martyr, and now the leader of the restored Christian church has suffered similar persecution, and has similarly become a martyr."

"Yes," interjected Borga, "and there is another similarity. The Council of Twelve Apostles is, as promised by Brigham Young, to carry on the work of the church and build on the foundation laid by the Prophet in the same way as did the Apostles of the original Christian church."

Changing the subject, Jens Pedersen wanted to know, "Has Governor Ford taken steps to prosecute the murderers of the Prophet?"

"I think they will go through the motions, but we all know what the verdict will be, since the judge is anti-Mormon, as well as the jurors," answered Caleb solemnly.

Borga reported, "We are in serious trouble again. Jens and I have made several trips to nearby towns to listen and find out all we could about the mood of the non-Mormons. We can tell you that it is ugly. I think that it will not be long before the Mormons will be forced to leave Nauvoo."

Brigham Young felt that the Saints needed something to boost their morale. He felt that the completion of the Temple was of prime importance as a means of giving courage to the Saints. Even before the Temple was completed, however, he announced that the Mormons were leaving Nauvoo. He felt that the announce-ment would pacify the non-Mormons and give the Saint time for orderly departure. But the pressure from the Gentiles was increasing as the Saints frantically made preparations to leave.

The Saints were getting organized for the trek west. Some of the families were given permission to travel as a subunit, known as the Danish Unit, even though Caleb was originally from Wales. At the first meeting of the group in preparation for their departure, Caleb was selected as their leader, and plans for their departure were drawn up. Caleb had discussed these plans with the men and summarized their conclusions.

"The men must continue to work two days a week on the Temple. We will cooperate in building three well-equipped wagons. Brother Borga Nielsen will be in charge of that activity. Jens will look after procurement of materials. We must dispose of our property and seek buyers at the best price we can get. Borga will be responsible for that. It will be necessary for you Sisters to plan food, clothing, and medicines."

At the next meeting of the group, Caleb asked Borga to report. "Jens and I have found a very serious situation on our scouting trips," Borga said. "The hostility is becoming bad. All kinds of charges are being made. They accuse the Mormons of not allowing non-Mormons to indulge in their accustomed vices while in Nauvoo, which seems very curious.

"Well," chimed in Jens, "it is true there are no taverns or brothels in our city."

"The life of President Young," continued Borga, "is now in real danger."

"Yes," said Caleb. "Brother Brigham is aware of this and is hastening to depart."

"There is another aspect to this," added Borga. "I find much property being offered for sale and buyers are holding out. They feel certain that they will be able to buy at bargain prices. It looks as if we will realize only a fraction of the worth of our property."

"Do you have any word, Brother Caleb, as to when we are apt to depart?" asked Jens.

"It appears tentatively," answered Caleb, "that Brigham Young will depart with the first group about the middle of February."

"That," stated Borga's father, "gives us only six weeks, if we leave with the first contingent. I believe we can have the wagons ready if the materials arrive. What is the situation there, Jens?"

"All timbers, iron and other hardware are available. We have a forge and an anvil; and some extra iron and coke to take along to make repairs."

"I have most of the required livestock lined up," announced Caleb, "subject to your approval."

"How are the Sisters' plans progressing, Borga?"

"They have made detailed plans for clothing and are working hard on preparing warm outfits. Plans for food have been made for each family. Within two weeks all the plans should be completed."

"It is not necessary," announced Caleb, "that we leave with the first contingent, but I hope that we can. We will meet again in two weeks to take stock of our preparations."

Detailed plans were announced for the exodus of the Mormons from Nauvoo. They were organized along military lines and operation was to be conducted as such. They were to depart in groups of sufficient size for mutual protection, but not so large as to overtax facilities.

"Let each company," the directive said, "prepare houses and fields at stations along the way for raising grain for those who are to follow later." Then, it continued: "Let every man use all his influence and property to remove these people to the place where the Lord shall locate a state of Zion."

At the next meeting of the Danish group it was announced that all property had been sold, but at a fraction of its value, and that all preparations were ready for leaving.

Permission had been obtained to accompany the first unit of 2,000 who were to leave with Brigham Young.

10

Borga had always gotten satisfaction when he discussed his problems with his mother. She was always a kind, intelligent and sympathetic listener. This evening, after the rest of the family had gone to bed, Christine remarked, "Borga, you look troubled. Are you feeling ill, or has something gone wrong?"

"No, Mother. Nothing physical, but I am bothered. You'll recall I gave considerable study to the Norse and Greek mythology, and the Bible in relation to our national religion. I wondered about the difference between mythology and religion, and whether our minister really had any divine authority?"

"Yes," said his mother. "I recall the questions you raised, and I was pleased when you thought that you had found satisfaction and some of the answers in the Prophet Joseph Smith's teachings."

"I've accepted the Prophet's teachings as the word of God, and no one can question my loyalty to Joseph Smith or to Brigham Young. I shall maintain that loyalty as we seek our land in the West, but I do have many unanswered questions."

"Perhaps you'll have more time and get your answers to them when we get out to our new home."

Christine hesitated, uncertain whether to bring the subject up, but then decided to go ahead.

"Don't you think, Borga, that it's time that you considered marriage?"

"Perhaps so, but I've been too busy to think much about the subject. There's really only one girl that has interested me, and she arrived on the *Maid of Iowa* with you and Father."

"Well, Borga," said Christine, as if she hadn't noticed his feelings toward Ethel, "she is a beautiful, intelligent girl. Why do you hesitate?"

"I don't think I could devote adequate attention to such matters until we arrive at our new home in the West, and by then it may be too late."

He hadn't solved any problems, but he felt better and more satisfied after talking with his mother. Borga wished he had more opportunity to study, to clarify his thinking, but this must wait. He realized that far more urgent, as well as more mundane tasks of survival on their western trek, must take priority.

The next morning Borga casually inquired of his sister Hedvig. "Have the Evans family decided how soon they will leave?"

"Brother Evans tried," said Hedvig, "to get permission to leave with us on the first contingent, but he has been asked to wait for the next one, about a month later. It would be so nice if they could leave with us."

"Is the delay because they are not ready?"

"No, they are ready and would like to start, but others in the group to which they have been assigned are not ready."

Borga decided to mention this situation casually to Caleb since he was on the High Council and had sympathetic interests in the Evans family because of their being Welsh like himself. Caleb discussed the situation with the authorities, with Mr. Evans and with Jens, and Borga's father, and it was decided that the Evans family should join them in the first contingent to leave.

It was twelve degrees below zero on February 15, as the first contingent headed west across the Mississippi River. The ice was thick enough to carry the heavy loads. The progress was slow and dangerous as they moved up the Iowa Bluffs on the west bank of the Mississippi River. Emotions were divided between sadness, as they looked back with sorrow at the beautiful city which they had built and were now being forced to leave, and a vague hope as they looked forward to their new home somewhere out west. The plan laid out by Brigham Young called for some to halt along the way at stations where they would build shelters, prepare ground and plant crops for those who would arrive later. Meetings were held after dinner whenever practical. These were always open and closed with prayer; some announcements were made and there was always singing.

The second day out in Iowa found them in six inches of snow, with very little grass for animals. After the animals were given a small ration of corn they were forced to browse on bark and twigs from the trees.

On the evening of the fifth day the complete contingent was ordered to halt, and the men were directed to gather wood so that a large campfire could be lighted. The people came shivering from their camps and surrounded the fire. All sang as the brass band played.

Borga, standing with Hedvig and Ethel, marveled at the effect that music, singing and close companionship had on the spirit of the people. After the closing prayer, the members walked toward their camps with a sprightlier step.

The next morning appeared to be utter confusion as the Saints got under way with all sorts of wagons and animals. Borga kept a rather tight rein on the group. He wanted it to be an orderly, well-run unit. Hedvig, Ethel and Borga were freer from family responsibilities than the others, so they joined in helping with any jobs which needed doing.

In the afternoon Borga rode ahead to see what the condition was of those along the line. He found some distressing sights. Two wagons were stalled in the mud. The first wagon was in a hole and the driver was beating his oxen. The animals were so weak that they couldn't budge the wagon. Borga called to him, "Brother, it won't do any good to beat those oxen. Why don't you get this man behind to double up with you?"

The driver stood dejected, "If I have to do that every time I get stuck in a mudhole, I had just as well stop right here."

The man in the second wagon sat listlessly on his wagon with little concern as to what happened next as Borga requested. "Get down and bring your oxen to help this first wagon out of the hole."

He reluctantly complied. After both wagons were through the home, Borga rode on. He thought, neither the men or their oxen had enough energy or spirit to go on. He found many in as poor condition. They had left either out of fear or ignorance, almost totally unprepared.

A couple of nights later it was Borga's turn to do guard duty. At about one o'clock in the morning he heard a disturbance. Investigating, he found a man attempting to steal something. He, with his gun ready, interrupted the man. With his hands held high the man begged Borga not to shoot. "My family hasn't had any food all day, and I felt that I had to get some, even if I had to steal it."

Borga gave him some food but warned him, "No stealing will be tolerated here. I will have to report you to the authorities in the morning."

It was quite obvious that unless they pushed on as fast as possible their provisions would be depleted. During April and May, however, the traveling was much easier and soon the livestock had plenty of food, and the spirits of the people were much lighter. They reached the bank of the Missouri River early in June.

Borga was enjoying the beautiful spring weather and the countryside as he rode over the prairie rounding up the cattle. His horse stepped in a hole and threw him, breaking his right arm. Brother Caleb, who had had some experience in first aid, set the arm, placed the splints, and bound it up.

Two weeks after this incident, an officer of the United States Army visited President Young with news that the Mormons would be requested to furnish five hundred men as soldiers to fight in the Mexican War, which had just broken out. This number of men from the Mormons was all out of proportion to the requirements put on other Americans, but the Mormons had no choice. It was quite clear that it was a continuation of the persecution of the Mormons. The five hundred men were furnished.

Out of the group, Jens, Caleb and Borga's father were requested to sign up for military duty. Brother Evans was not well. Gustaf, Jens' adopted son, was too young and Borga had a broken arm. At the time the men were to leave a party was held, to help dispel the grief. Having to send the men to war after just having been driven out of Nauvoo and having made the long, muddy trek across Iowa, was almost too much.

The women, however, dressed in their best. The meeting opened with prayer. There was music, singing, food and some laughter—and copious tears. There was more gaiety than might be expected, however, under the conditions. As the men marched off, Borga felt weighted down with his added responsibilities.

The west side of the Missouri River was Indian Territory. Brigham Young made an agreement with Chief Big Elk, of the Omaha Indians, for the Mormons to build a temporary city which they called Winter Quarters, and which was to serve those already there as well as those who would come later.

The city was laid out with streets and water supply, a flour mill and sawmill. Many houses were constructed and repairs were made to wagons and equipment; and crops were planted.

All the Saints at Winter Quarters were continually urged by the church leaders to hold regular church services. Prayers and speeches were made by members of the church, admonishing the folks in the community as to what should be done and what should not be done; emphasizing what was wrong and what was right; urging all to help each other. There was always a great deal of singing of religious songs, and the meetings always began and ended with prayer.

All were encouraged to sing at campfires and in their homes; also, many dancing groups were organized. Those offering the prayers as well as the speakers were "called" to do so by the Bishop. In many cases they were not asked until they arrived in church.

Borga was particularly interested in the men who played the fiddles and called for the dances at the same time. In Denmark he had seen a lot of folk dancing, but he had not seen anything like the dancing in Winter Quarters, with the fiddlers calling movements of the dances. Everyone joined in the activities and seemed to have a gay time, even after a hard day's work—and the awareness of another hard one ahead the next morning.

One evening in discussion with his mother, Borga commented, "In listening to the various speeches of Brigham Young, I am impressed with the difference between him and Joseph Smith."

"In what way do you mean, Borga?"

"Joseph was emotional, issued many revelations which he claimed God had commanded him to reveal. Suffering experienced by the Saints was often attributed by him to the action of God as being a test of their faithfulness."

"And what about Brigham?" asked his mother.

"He shows very little emotion. He does not seem certain whether he is issuing a revelation from God or whether it is his own conclusions arrived at by reasoning. Suffering of the Saints is more apt to be attributed, by him, to lack of using good sense, or lack of sufficient labor. His advice is always of a very practical nature."

"Which seems to impress you most, Borga?"

"Possibly there are different methods of arriving at and using visions. Joseph and Brigham translated visions into acts—each by his own method: Joseph, as a prophet, and Brigham as a practical leader. Others may refer to such ideas as the still small voice, the hearts open to conviction, and the soul. All seemed to be trying to interpret nature as they observe it."

"My goodness, Borga," cautioned Christine, "remember, I cannot swim. Please do not get me into the water which is too deep."

Borga chuckled. "Perhaps you are right, Mother—at least, until I improve my own ability to swim myself."

Ethel had become a very devoted member of the church. She was by nature a cheerful girl, and she got much joy out of her church work, and out of her studies of the Bible and the *Book of Mormon*.

A large amount of sickness and death that occurred since the Mormons arrived in Winter Quarters had required much help from those capable of giving it. She had good health and was happy to give more than her share to help others who needed it.

After three months of this, however, she found herself a bit weary, and with a tendency to brood. This Sunday after returning from church she went to her room. As she lay on her bed her mind ran back over her recent experiences.

Her parents were very poor in their native Wales, and she had very little formal education. Through her strong desire to improve herself she had obtained work at the age of fourteen with a Mr. and Mrs. Parsons to help Mrs. Parsons care of her two children.

Mr. Parsons was from London but had extensive financial holdings in Wales. Ethel accompanied them during the summer as Mr. Parsons travelled about Wales.

They treated her well but kept her at arm's length. They didn't want her to forget that she was their servant. They took her to London the following winter. The year with them, she felt, had been a valuable education which she could hardly have gotten in any other way. They seemed anxious to have her stay with them, but she realized that she was in a niche there from which she was not likely to escape if she stayed with them.

She and her parents had listened to some Mormon missionaries several times prior to her work with the Parsons. Ethel had been in touch with her parents by letter and it had been decided that they would emigrate from Wales to the United States and join the Mormon church.

She had experienced many hardships since leaving Wales but they had not dampened her spirit. What did the future hold for her? Would she ever have a happy home of her own?

With the Mormon group there was only one man for whom she had any real fondness. He seemed to take little notice of her, although he was always kind and respectful. She took hope, however, in the fact that he seemed not to have an interest in any other woman. She realized that he was a very conscientious person and that there was always more work to be done at Winter Quarters than there were able-bodied men to do it. Perhaps as things settled down life would become a little easier and there would be more opportunity for the more romantic side of life.

Next Sunday in the afternoon meeting, the speaker chastised those who allowed themselves to become depressed. Ethel was taking it to heart and apparently showing her feelings more than she realized. As church dismissed, she was standing alone observing some children running around among the audience outside. Suddenly she realized that someone was standing behind her. Borga had walked up. "Happy?" he whispered in her ear.

She gave a sign, which was an answer in itself. "Very much so."

"I was watching you in church," said Borga, "and I thought you looked as if something were troubling you."

"Oh, I didn't realize that I was showing my feelings so. It was nothing of any importance," she insisted. "I suppose my conscience may have bothered me for allowing my ugly self to become slightly depressed."

"You shouldn't be surprised at that; each of us can be several people all in one. Most of us have at least two personalities."

"Do you?" she inquired as she watched his eyes.

Borga got a chuckle out of her question. "I certainly do. Some nice and some mean."

"I don't believe that," she said. "I doubt that any of you are mean."

"Don't you?" He was watching her expression. "It is true, nevertheless. Not that I am proud to admit it, but you seem to have a way of making me face the music."

"That is a big subject." He was fumbling with some papers held in his hands, as he continued "too big and too serious for such a beautiful day as this."

They walked away from the church together as he continued to talk. "But on one thing I can assure you—the me that has had the pleasure of being friends with you is the nicest me. It is probably better if you never have to meet the other."

He looked rather serious she thought as he took her hand to help her across the brook on the way home. He held on to her hand much longer, she noted, than was necessary to get across the brook.

As they parted Ethel recalled that Borga had on many occasions shown some indications that he liked her, but they were so subtle that she was never sure. She was thrilled at the assurance she got out of the simple act of his holding her hand as they walked home.

When she was alone, she laughed and then was serious as she thought of the different Borgas which he mentioned. She knew that she liked the nice one, but she wondered about the others. She thought surely, though, that they could not be very bad.

It was now early spring at Winter Quarters and much had been accomplished since the Saints arrived there one year earlier. There was talk of a party leaving for the Rocky Mountains soon. The snow had melted leaving bare ground over most of the area, and even a little fresh grass was showing along the brooks.

It was Sunday and Borga called at her home for Ethel to go to the afternoon fast meetings. As the services were opened for testimony many of the members arose and confirmed their knowledge of the truthfulness of the gospel.

Borga was a little nervous as Ethel arose to speak. "My dear Brothers and Sisters: I feel that I should take this opportunity to express my gratitude to God and to my family and to you for the privilege of being in your midst and sharing with you this wonderful gospel of the *Latter-Day Saints*. I am grateful for the knowledge I have of the truthfulness of the Gospel.

"I know that it is God's word and that this church is the only true Christian church. I know that Joseph Smith was a true prophet of God, that he saw and spoke with God and that the *Book of Mormon* as translated from the *Golden Plates* by Joseph Smith, is the history of the early peoples of this continent.

"I pray with all my heart that I may live so that I shall be permitted to marry in the Temple to the husband of my choice for time and all eternity. I pray that I will be a good wife and mother, and that I may raise children according to the principles of this church. I pray for a happy and useful life with my future family. I am grateful that I have been given the opportunity, if I live according to the principles of the church, to go to the Temple and have my future husband and children sealed to me for life and eternity.

"I feel well repaid for any hardship I have experienced in emigrating to this country to join the church. I feel very humble and beg your forgiveness if I have done anything to hurt anyone's feelings, or to bring displeasure in the sight of God. These things I pray for in the name of Jesus Christ, Amen."

Borga was very conscious of Ethel's tremor, and felt her emotional strain when she sat down.

He had been asked to speak at the evening services, so he walked home with Ethel and then went to his home to think about what he would say in church that evening.

Just prior to the meeting he called for Ethel again, and they walked to church. Borga was asked to come to the front and sit facing the audience. His speech was to be short, announced the Bishop since other business was to follow. He was well known to most of the audience. Many of the women had made some whispering remarks recently as Borga and Ethel had been seen together several times.

In Borga's speech he called attention to what he thought was one of the most potent principles that Joseph Smith had announced. "Man is that he might have joy." This, he thought, gave buoyancy and hope. He related this to another principle announced by the Prophet "Man is as God once was, and as God is man may become." He called their attention to the celestial glory that Joseph visualized, if the Mormons lived according to the commandments of God.

He contrasted this concept with early Norse mythological concepts. The mythology or religion of the early Norsemen was very harsh. Asgard, the home of the Gods, was an ugly, disagreeable heaven as was Valhalla, the hall of Asgard, to which the heroes and the heroines who braved death were entitled to go. The Gods, the heroes, as well as their heavenly home, were always doomed to destruction.

They, like the forces of good, struggled hopelessly against adversity, but even so the Gods and heroes fought on. They never yielded. This idea permeated all Norse mythology, and it certainly was a gloomy conception. The only support for the drooping human spirit that honorable men could hope for was heroism for causes which had lost their purpose.

Asgard was very severe, even though the attendant maidens, the Valkyries, kept the drinking horns full at Valhalla. Their chief function, as set by the god Odin, was to decide on the battlefield those who were to win and die. They were then to carry the brave dead back to Odin in Valhalla to the special chamber in Asgard which was reserved for the heroes. The heroes always died.

After Borga had completed his discussion, the Bishop complimented him on his speech, and then made an announce-ment.

President Young would leave for the Rocky Mountains on the 16th of April, just two weeks later. It had been decided that the party should be made up almost completely of able-bodied men now in Winter Quarters, with only three women being allowed to go. He would select the men within a few days. All men were urged to make themselves ready in case they might be selected.

11

On Tuesday morning, just as the sun was coming up, Ethel was walking through the pasture toward the milk cow. She had a milk pail on her arm and she was singing. She especially enjoyed the early mornings when the dew still glistened on the fields, and the birds seemed especially lively. The woods and the field seemed to have a special meaning at this time of day. The sun, as it passed through her hair, gave a varied brilliance to its dark red color.

She was startled by a call from between some shrubs along the roadway.

"Who is it?" she called, not quite recognizing the person.

"It's me. I'm enjoying the impromptu performance. Do you often do this?" he asked, as he came toward her.

"Oh, hello, Borga," she called, going to meet him. "What are you doing here this time of the morning?"

"Some cattle got out, and I've been rounding them up."

He looked ruggedly attractive, she thought, even though he needed a shave.

"Was I acting absurdly childish out there in the fields?" she asked.

"No, you were gay, natural and really charming." He was amused at the color that flushed to her face. "You are not used to such compliments," he teased.

"It's because I get so few. I don't seem to attract some men, and some are not attractive to me."

"Don't you have any romantic ambitions?"

She laughed. "I probably couldn't convince anyone who had heard my little talk in church last Sunday that I didn't have some hopes, provided the right man came along."

"Well," he said, "that could be quite a challenge to some man."

Borga was rather disconcerting in a number of ways, Ethel thought. He was quite different than most of the men she knew.

She was sure that she didn't understand him fully, but he fascinated her. She was a little uncomfortable at the way he was looking at her.

"Next Sunday," he said, "is the last time I'll be able to see you before I leave. I would like to make a date for church in the evening. After church, I have some philosophy I would like to discuss with you."

"That will be fine, Borga. Are you going to get me into deep water?"

"You never can tell, Ethel," he remarked in a light mood. "In these uncertain and somewhat dangerous times we are living, we must consider all problems which confront us. I'll see you Sunday evening," he said, riding away.

Borga had spent some of the best years of his young life in the defense of the Mormon church. He admired the Mormon people. There were some bad apples in the bag but that had to be expected, considering the present state of human development. He had nothing to show for it except his own self-respect.

He had killed four men in battle in defense of his fellow Mormons. This weighed heavily on his conscience, but he was determined not to let it get him down. He, likewise, vowed that it would not dull his humanitarian sensitivities.

Borga was essentially self-educated, but both while he was growing up in Denmark, as well as since he joined the Mormon church, he had followed the advice of his grandfather and his parents to read widely.

He recalled that some form of man has been in existence on earth for probably one million years. Man started writing history about six thousand years ago. He has been able to write in only the last fraction of one per cent of the time that he has been on earth.

Man, since his development to the stage where he could think well enough to write, or at least to where he had left written records, had in his mythology, astrology and religion postulated gods and goddesses, or their equivalent, in many forms.

This helped to justify his curiosity about a life before this one and a life after this one, as well as for the control of natural phenomena. Various rituals have been invented or established around these hypotheses, the practice of which has tended to make people not realize that the ideas were once based consciously or unconsciously on unverified hypotheses.

The concepts were either never recognized as hypotheses, or else that fact has been lost in history. They were given in the case of religion as revelations by Prophets or other religious leaders. After hearing these ideas expressed many times people seemed to arrive at a state wherein they were convinced the truthfulness of the ideas. Borga had truly read widely—and wisely.

Borga had never admitted to Ethel that he loved her, although he had known it himself since he first met her as she landed from the *Maid of Iowa* that 4th of July in Nauvoo. He always outwardly indicated that he was too busy to get involved with romantic affairs, but there was a secret reason. He did not want to hurt her and was afraid that some of his thinking would greatly disturb her.

He felt now, however, that out of fairness to Ethel he must let her know that he loved her, and, of course, hoped she might love him. Because of the uncertainty of the future for both of them, he could not ask her to wait for him. He would, he concluded, express his love for her before he left for the Rocky Mountains, and if she responded favorably, they would have to rely on hope for a reunion in the future somewhere out west.

On Sunday evening, as they walked home after church, he held her hand and they both secretly realized that they were talking about things other than what they both wished to discuss. When they arrived at Ethel's home, he took both her hands, and Ethel said in a light mood, "What about the philosophy you mentioned the other morning, that you were going to discuss with me tonight?"

He gave a slightly chagrined laugh. "I'm afraid I stretched things a little when I called it philosophy. But if it can be called that it is a very practical variety that affects both of us intimately. I can honestly say, Ethel darling, that I never had loved any girl until I first met you, and since then I have continued to love only you."

Her hands had moved to his shoulders and then were around his neck as he pulled her to him, and they kissed in strong emotion, such as neither had ever experienced before.

"Oh Borga," she said, as she pushed herself away so she could talk to him. "I could repeat what you have said by changing only the word *girl* to *boy*."

"Our lives are so uncertain," said Borga, "that I will not ask you to wait for me. But I hope with all my heart that we will be able to continue our relations as we meet again out west."

They were in each other's arms again and Ethel assured him, "No engagement is necessary. Our mutual love is all we need."

12

After much preparation, the company of Mormons pulled out of Winter Quarters and headed west on April 16, 1847. It consisted of 143 men, 3 women and 2 children; 72 wagons, 93 horses, 52 mules, 66 oxen, 19 cows, 17 dogs and quite a considerable number of chickens. The men all carried rifles and small weapons. In their wagons was an assortment of agricultural implements, such as plows, as well as implements for building and setting up flour mills and sawmills. Besides provisions for one year, the wagons contained an adequate supply of various seeds, including especially grain seed.

Strict discipline was maintained all along the march. The bugle awakened them at 5:00 o'clock in the morning. After prayer and breakfast, camp was broken up and they were on their way within an hour. Before sundown each night the wagons were pulled into a circle and the cattle were driven inside, this serving as a corral and as a fort in case of Indian attack. Many Indians could be seen along the way in the distance; some of them followed the caravan and there was always uncertainty as to what might happen.

Borga was assigned as a scout. These men took turns riding horseback ahead of the wagon trains. They were keen observers and had above-average intelligence. Their task was to observe the terrain, watch out for enemy Indians who might attack; look for indications of recent tracks of Indians; look for proper places and directions which appeared most likely available for easy travel; and to look for suitable campsites. This task also required finding places where food could be obtained for the animals, and thus, also, watering places for cattle and for people.

On this particular day Borga had set out without food deliberately because he wanted to try to live off the land. As he rode off ahead of the wagon train, he had a can of water and some salt. Anything else he must glean from the land until he met the wagon train again in the evening.

As he was riding along, he thought that he might be near some Indians without knowing it. He must avoid attracting their attention wherever possible, especially since he was out alone and the territory was entirely new.

He recalled that some dry plants develop smoke when used to start a fire. This can be immediately detected by the Indians. For building fires, one should choose a material that did not throw smoke easily, he concluded. Buffalo chips would not be good for this use, although they were sometimes convenient and useful.

He must select material, if he wished to build a fire, which would give out little smoke, and the fire should be only as large as needed to do his cooking. He would do this under trees so that as the smoke passed up through the trees it would diffuse and would be less easily detected.

In the early spring certain plants were available for food. Borga was aware that there were two different kinds of sego lilies. One plant looked like a small onion and the other had a much broader leaf. Both of these plants belonged to the lily family, but one is poisonous and the other one was edible. He sharpened a stick so that he could dig up the bulb, located about four or five inches below the surface, and he found them quite tasty.

After lunch, as he rode, he thought about the animals or birds he saw on his way. The type of animal life sometimes told an observer what was apt to be near. There was a killdeer on the ground. It was rare that one found one of these birds far from water. He noted the possible existence of a fault which he had seen earlier and decided to move in that direction.

Not far away there was a large grassy area which would make an excellent campsite. On closer examination he found a small brook and following it up he found it was a spring with large cottonwood trees growing near it, and there were many willows. What an excellent campsite this will be for the wagon train tonight, he thought; but before he decided, he observed the surrounding area to see if he could detect the presence of any Indians who might attack.

He spent an hour exploring the surrounding area and then he decided that there was no indication of Indians in the neighborhood. He had left prearranged plans or directions along the path for the wagon trains, and since he had found no reason for changing the direction, he would not need to ride back and meet it.

He must get everything lined up so that when the wagon trains arrived, they would know pretty well what to do. As usual the entrance plans of the wagons were precisely outlined with a definite circle to surround the entire area for protection of the livestock, as well as possible attack from Indians. The wagon train was not expected for the next two hours, and his job was to get enough wood gathered for the night. He was sure the folks would be exhausted from their long trek by the time they reached this area.

The Mormon group arrived that night, exhausted but pleased with the campsite Borga had prepared for them.

13

Many streams had to be forded during the trek west. The Platte River had already been crossed once. About one hundred miles west of Laramie, Borga, while on one of his scouting trips, came to a place on the Platte River where it looked as if they would certainly have to cross it again.

Because of the spring rains and the warmer weather, the river was at flood stage. He explored several possible places where the fording might take place. However, each time he rode his horse in to find the depth of water he found his mount swimming.

After deciding that it seemed almost certain that the water was too deep for normal fording, he swam his mount across the river to explore the other side. He could find no place where fording seemed possible.

This information was passed back to the wagon train and it was decided that the wagons would have to be unloaded and their burden placed in boats made of skin and floated across the river. Then the wagons would have to be pulled across and all the livestock would have to be forced to swim across. When they got to the other side the wagons would, of course, have to be reloaded. This took lots of work and much delay.

When the wagon train arrived in Green River, Wyoming, Brigham Young met Samuel Brannan who had led a branch of the church from New York around the Horn to California by sailing ship. The trip from New York to San Francisco had taken nearly six months. Several stops had been made along the route. Brannan had come east from San Francisco, where he had established his colony.

Brannan tried to persuade Young to go on to California. But Young had decided definitely that he would not go. The Saints should settle in the mountains where they would be safer from the persecutions similar to what they had experienced in the east.

Brigham Young was afraid that if they went on to San Francisco, many more people would follow and that the same type of persecution might be experienced as in Missouri and elsewhere.

One of the inducements that Brannan offered was that he had received word the Mormon Battalion had arrived at the Pueblo de Los Angeles and that it would be easy to collect the members of the battalion in California. Brigham Young appreciated this suggestion from Brannan but pointed out that the Brannan group had not experienced the persecutions suffered by the Saints in Ohio, Missouri, and Illinois.

About this time the scouts made contact with two mountain men associated with the fur-trapping industries. Somewhat conflicting information relative to the best places for location and the routes into the Salt Lake Valley were obtained from Peg Leg Smith and Jim Bridger. Bridger did not have much favorable comment about the possibility of a profitable settlement in the Great Salt Lake Valley. In fact, he painted a dim picture. He did, however, give them directions for the shortest route into the valley.

Peg Leg Smith thought a better location would be to the north in what was called Cache Valley by the mountain men, since this was where they cached their furs and had made a winter rendezvous.

Brigham Young decided to take the shortest route into the valley, and a group of scouts was sent out to explore this route. Borga and two other scouts, however, got permission to explore the route through Cache Valley. They would then meet the main company as it arrived in Salt Lake Valley and report their findings.

Borga and his two companions were on horseback and, of course, could move relatively fast. They explored Cache Valley and Bear River Valley and then moved south into the Great Salt Lake basin, arriving on July 20, where they anticipated that the wagon train would come. The wagon train had found rough going, even though the route was comparatively short, and did not arrive until July 24.

Borga and his companions reported that they found Cache Valley and Bear River Valley in the north to be very beautiful and had considerable promise for suitable locations. Brigham Young was firm, however, and corralled the wagons near the mouth of what was later called City Creek Canyon, which was approximately what is now known as Salt Lake City.

Within days the location of a temple site was made. Organization of farms were laid out and planted to potatoes, turnips and grain. Ditches were dug so that these crops could be irrigated. Other groups were organized to explore the mountains for timber locations, for dams and mills. Another group was set up to explore thoroughly the northern valleys of Cache and Bear River.

The territory on which the Mormons intended to locate did not at that time belong to the United States, but rather was held as Mexican territory. It was later ceded to the United States at the Treaty of Guadalupe-Hildago, which ended the Mexican War. The Mormons did not have legal right to the territory there and did not acquire it until much later.

Shortly after Borga had completed clearing the land assigned to the group and had it planted to grain, he was dispatched with two other companions to California. They left on horseback, with the task of procuring wagons and horses to bring back a supply of seed for grain, fruit, vegetables, as well as some implements. They were expected to return late in the fall.

14

Just before the second wagon train was to leave Winter Quarters the members of the group were confronted with some disagreeable news. It particularly affected the Danewal portion of the wagon train. It had become evident that Jenny Jones, Caleb's second wife, who had no children, was pregnant. Caleb had been gone with the Mormon battalion for more than a year. There was speculation as to who the father was, but Jenny would not talk. Brother Evans tried to get her to confess and try to make things better for all, including herself and her baby, but to no avail. It caused much uncomfortable feeling during the entire trip west.

Caleb's first wife, Clara, was the most upset in the group. She became quite ill and was hardly able to take care of her children during most of the trip.

Christine took sick one day along the route. Apparently, she had eaten some bad food and, unknown to the rest of the group, she had strayed from the train. Before she was aware of it, they were out of sight, and she could not call to them. She began to walk but became so faint that she decided to sit down and hope for the best. Little Carl was in her arms, and he had become too heavy. She was not strong enough to carry him very far.

It was about 3:00 o'clock in the afternoon when Hedvig noticed her mother's absence. An immediate search was made of the entire train and there was no trace of her. Two men were assigned to go on horseback along the route that had been followed.

Just before dark they found her. She had practically given up hope and had settled down to die on the prairie. One of the men took Carl with him. Christine was placed in the saddle on another horse, and a man rode behind and helped to steady her during the trip. They arrived back in camp at midnight, where everyone eagerly awaited them.

58

The early part of the trip through Nebraska and eastern Wyoming was pleasant. The grass was green, giving plenty of food for the livestock. But the trip through western Wyoming and into the Salt Lake Valley was hot, dry and dusty.

They arrived in the valley in late August, after considerable sickness and a number of deaths along the way. The valley, when they arrived, did not look very attractive to the travelers at that time of the year. Everything was dry, and little timber could be seen anywhere near the fort that had been started.

Although the conditions under which they were living in Salt Lake Valley left much to be desired, Brigham Young sent word back with Captain Brown to members of the Mormon battalion in California that every possible care was being taken to make life as comfortable as possible for the families of the Mormon battalion. Members of the battalion were urged to stay in California for a year, find work, and save money for use when they returned to Salt Lake Valley.

The temporary quarters to which they were assigned were under construction inside the fort, which had been started upon the arrival of the first company. The walls of the fort were made of adobe, and the houses being constructed were inside these walls. The sides of the houses were made of aspen poles laid horizontally, and the roof was flat. It was constructed by first placing large supporting poles horizontally about two feet apart, then covering these with willows at right angles to the larger poles.

On top of the willows was placed fine straw, weeds and rushes of whatever nature they could find. This in turn was covered with earth. There was little time to construct anything better before winter. This worked quite well for most of the winter and kept them not too uncomfortable. But as they found out later, when the snow began to melt in the Spring, the flat roof, as they had constructed it, was not the proper kind for the territory. They spent much of their time dodging the dropping water inside their houses. Much of this, of course, was corrected for the next winter.

One building lot was assigned to each family on what was called South Main Street. The street was laid out 125 feet wide. Each lot was four rods wide and ten rods deep. These were considered permanent assignments on which future homes could be built. In addition to this, each family was assigned two acres of ground farther back from the street. The latter areas were assigned to the members for food production. Any excess food which each family could produce in these areas could be turned into the bishop's storehouse for which, along with any wages received for public work, credit was given.

Work and industry were always stressed in the Mormon church, along with the more religious matters. There was an off-the-record expression heard often, "We pray fervently and frequently, but we always go out and work like hell to make our prayers yield results." The idea was always stressed that, "Faith without work is fruitless." The beehive was chosen by the Mormons as their emblem, representing industry and cooperation.

At the bishop's storehouse members could, with whatever credits they had earned, buy clothing, food, seeds and implements, as long as these things were available. Dry goods, such as clothing and quilts, were made by the women and turned into the store-house as a public service. These could be purchased by those who could afford them and were furnished free to those who were unable to pay.

Early in the church history the women were organized into activity which was known as the Relief Society. No women could hold the priesthood. Their function was to work closely with the bishop in helping any needy families, in case of hardship. Practically every woman was expected to work in this organization. They not only helped in case of illness, but they made clothing, quilts, and had regular meetings at which they discussed matters pertinent to the home, especially in relation to the teachings of the Mormon Church.

When any illness struck a home in the ward, the president of the relief societies would see that some of the sisters were sent there to help. Also, when a death occurred in a family, the relief society sisters would take over and see that the proper things were done regarding the body of the deceased.

They would prepare the corpse, dress it according to what was regarded as the proper type of dress, and also provide for the family's food and care during the days immediately preceding and following the funeral. Much was done to ease the grief of the mourning family.

The families lived close together and congeniality was the order of the day. This precious bond was probably strengthened by the fact that three, and sometimes four, of the men folk were away during the first year at Salt Lake Valley and staying together under close friendship furnished mutual support.

Upon arrival in Salt Lake Valley each family of the group had one team of oxen, and some had a cow and calf. Some had a horse for riding.

Borga was able to clear all the land assigned to the families and plant the wheat before he left for California. The wheat sprouted with the early fall rains, and by spring they had bountiful crops.

15

Up to now, the Mormons had had little time to think of Christmas festivities. This year Hedvig was anxious for their families to celebrate this important holiday. She wanted Gustaf to help her, but there was no money and so they had to find other means to develop the Christmas spirit. One evening Gustaf noticed that Hedvig was doing something he did not understand. "What are you wasting your time at now?" he asked.

"Go away and mind your business. If you had a little more appreciation of the beautiful things of Christmas, you wouldn't ask such a silly question."

Considerable attention had been given recently in church to ideas relative to Christmas. It had taken root in Hedvig's mind with a vengeance.

They had never had a Christmas tree before and the idea seemed a little farfetched, but the more they thought and talked about it, the more they came to think that Hedvig's ideas were good. They decided to go to the Mountains and bring home a Christmas tree.

Gustaf had made several trips to the mountains for fence posts and timber but had not paid much attention to the kinds of evergreen trees growing in the area which might serve as Christmas trees.

The week before Christmas, Gustaf and Hedvig decided to make the trip. On both sides of City Creek Canyon could be seen evergreens in the mountains. The ground was covered with snow, and the trees were a few miles away; but, nevertheless, Gustaf and Hedvig were full of Christmas spirit and zeal. They headed for the area which seemed easiest, and where Gustaf remembered seeing some small trees which he thought would be suitable for yuletide.

Hedvig had definite ideas about the kind of tree that was suitable for Christmas. Not just any old kind of evergreen would do for her. The spruce or fir trees seemed the only trees suitable, according to her. She had learned this in some of her church activities. The trees at the first location they headed for were what were called junipers, and Hedvig assured Gustaf, when they got there that they were entirely unsuitable. She didn't seem to be certain as to the source of her knowledge about yule trees, but she was positive.

When they got down to the river, which was known as City Creek, they discovered that it was quite wide and that the water was deep in places. "This place looks as if the bottom is fairly smooth and the water not more than up to my waist," said Gustaf. "You carry the ax and our lunch, and I'll carry you on my back."

"I can make it by myself," said Hedvig, but Gustaf insisted and carried her across. He slipped, and they and their lunch were soaked in the river. But their spirits were not dampened, and they finally got to the trees. They walked fast in an attempt to keep from getting cold. Carefully, Gustaf selected the most perfect specimen, of course, with Hedvig's approval, and then dragged the tree over the snow to the river, along an old road leading to their home.

It had taken much longer than they had expected, and it was just getting dark as they arrived at the river's edge. It had turned very cold and their wet clothes were freezing on them. Hedvig had become chilled and kept wanting to stop and rest, but Gustaf was afraid to let her do so because there was danger of her freezing.

When they had not returned by dark a party was sent out to search for them. Their wagon and horses were found and the trail up the mountain was still visible. It had started to snow, and everyone was worried. One search party had followed their trail, and another one had come up the road. Hedvig and Gustaf met the search party about four miles from their home.

The next morning Hedvig felt very sick, and she ran a high temperature. She had to stay in bed until the day before Christmas. Gustaf made a stand for the tree and placed it in Hedvig's home. Ethel helped Hedvig decorate it. They had made gifts for all the children of the group. These were placed on the tree with the names of the children on them.

Everyone thought that it was the nicest Christmas they had ever experienced. The sad aspect of the occasion was that the fathers of most of the families were still in California, although they had been discharged from the army and were working there to earn some money to bring home.

16

Brigham Young advised all members of the church to be cautious in dealing with the Indians. They were to give them no opportunity to steal since, he explained, it was the nature of the Indian to steal. They steal from each other. He also instructed the members not to take revenge into their own hands. Any grievance should be taken up with the local Indian Chief, whenever a crime was committed.

Borga felt that the Indians had a real grievance against the Mormons and other whites. As the white people moved in and took over part of the land it limited the Indians' ability to live off the game from their land. It was natural that unless something else could be provided to take the place of this, there was bound to be serious problems arising.

He had done some trading with the Indians and had a few things of which he was quite proud. He had a buckskin jacket, which was made by the Indians, for which he traded some food.

The church continually encouraged participation in the activities, and all were continually being asked to make short speeches on any subject of their choice. Since Borga's sympathy had been aroused to some extent for justice toward the Indians, he decided that the next time he was asked, he would talk about this problem.

It was not long before he was asked to speak in church. At one point in his speech he said, "I feel that the Mormons are actually stealing from the Indians, and we are not giving them anything in return. I feel it is questionable ethics. We are concerning ourselves about the Indians stealing from us, and yet we are coming in and stealing land from the Indians, actually."

When he sat down after his short speech, the bishop arose from his chair and stated that he felt that Borga had created too much guilt feeling in the audience and he proceeded to explain that he appreciated Borga's feelings of justice for their brothers the Indians, but he also said that the Mormons must take a broader look than Borga had done.

God had commanded his people to go forth and multiply and replenish the earth and subdue it, and the Indians or Lamanites, as he called them, had departed from the Gospel in their wickedness and were not doing as God had commanded, and therefore, the Mormons must help them to do this.

In this way the Mormons were not stealing the land but were helping to bring enlightenment to the Lamanites and showing them how to use the land properly. Borga thought that this seemed to be a way of explaining away the Mormon guilt, but he did not say so.

The early pioneer experiences were demanding for all the people, frequently testing their initiative and self-reliance. The second summer in the Salt Lake Valley, Borga had planted alfalfa in a small piece of ground. He had had no experience with this crop but followed the instructions which he had been given by those who had had experience with it. Seed was very precious. It had been brought in from California to the valley, and only a small amount was given to each one to plant. It came up nicely and by early summer he had a good stand of alfalfa on these few square rods of ground.

He had arranged to get irrigation water and had a vigorous growth. Borga also had built a small corral in which to keep a cow and a fifteen-month-old heifer. Warning had been given him that ruminants, such as cows, which chew their cud, were subject to dangers when allowed to eat green foods of certain types, especially legumes. One of these was alfalfa. Under particular conditions when the green alfalfa, or similar types of food such as clover, were eaten rapidly by animals, a fermentation took place in the stomach of the animal and bloated it so quickly that the animal sometimes died.

Borga had had no experience with animals under these conditions. All he knew was what he had been told. He did not worry about it, however, because he thought that the corral fence that he had made was ample to restrain the animals from further movement.

But as he went out one morning to milk the cow, he found that his heifer had gotten out and was in the alfalfa patch. She had been hungry and had relished the green alfalfa. The growth was covered with dew, which made the condition most likely to cause damage to the animal. She seemed to be in serious trouble and was bloated badly. He pulled out his pocketknife and jabbed the blade into her side; gas escaped immediately, and he cut the opening big enough so that the alfalfa could be pulled out with his finger. The heifer relaxed from the spasms of pain and seemed to be resting peacefully. Hardly fifteen minutes had passed when she got up, walked around, and it was not long before she started to eat again.

After putting the heifer back in the corral, and repairing the fence, he went home feeling quite proud that he had been able to save the animal; but a little chagrined that he had not done a better job of making a fence.

17

It was a bright crisp morning and Borga was having a pleasant discussion with Ethel prior to the starting of Sunday school. Bishop Jenkins stopped and greeted them. "Brother Borga, would you mind stopping for a few minutes after Sunday school?" Then with a knowing twinkle, and a wink to Ethel, "I wouldn't want to interfere with any plans that you two lovely people have in mind."

"I won't let it, Borga," remarked Ethel with a laugh. "I'll wait right here."

"That's a good girl," said the bishop as he left.

"I wonder what he has in mind," queried Borga.

At the meeting, the bishop told Borga, "We feel the need of a new class for our advanced adults in Sunday school, and we think that you are just the man to lead such a class."

"This is indeed a surprise. I'm not sure that I'm the best choice for such a job. What are your thoughts as to the nature of the subject matter?"

"We have, in various meetings, been saying the same things in the same old way for quite a long time now. This is a good sound Mormon doctrine, but we think that a fresh approach will be stimulating. We are going to leave the subject matter, and the method of conducting the class, up to you. The class will be held each Sunday for a thirty-minute period, the same length as all the Sunday school classes. As you know we have an adult class now, but we think that there is a need for a class with a fresh approach."

"You have given me a dangerous assignment, Bishop."

"Borga, you have handled many dangerous assignments before. The only assignment that you have refused to take, that I'm aware of, is the taking of a wife. Now you had better go to that beautiful girl waiting for you."

As he left, he remarked, "Remember, Borga, you have to prepare for your advancement in the celestial kingdom."

Borga and Ethel went for a long walk up North Temple Street where they could look down over the entire settlement.

"Borga, I'm so happy that the bishop has selected you to do this. I think that you will do it very effectively."

"Ethel, I'm frightened. I want to think it over before finally deciding. There are some hazards to it."

"In what way do you mean?"

"You remember a long time back, Ethel, when we were speaking in a light mood about the number of individuals all combined in one? I told you that I had an ugly me. I think at least some may regard it as ugly. I've tried to repress it because it makes some persons unhappy, and this in turn makes me unhappy. The tendency I speak of is my desire to get all the information that I can on a subject, whether it is pleasant or unpleasant. Many persons like to select their information."

"Well, Borga, I don't see how that can get you into trouble in a class like the bishop wants you to lead."

"I hope you are right. But I have some doubts. What do you think would be a good way to start the class?"

"All the people here have gone through quite a lot of hardships, Borga. It would do us good to review, in a critical way, all the information available to us."

"Ethel, you have just suggested the name of the class. I'm going to call it a *Class Discussion of Information about our Church*."

Borga and Ethel were together at every opportunity now. As they walked to her home she remarked, "I feel so good tonight. In fact, I think I'm happier now that I have ever been."

Borga answered by getting her in his arms and kissing her vehemently.

Just before leaving Ethel at her home, he said, "Ethel, I have a secret that I have not divulged to anyone yet. I have been studying legal matters for some time. I have a fair library which I obtained in Nauvoo, and I want to prepare myself for the legal profession. I believe that there will be need for men with that training. Later, I may go somewhere to complete my studies."

"That is wonderful, Borga. I'm sure that you will do well at it."

Next Sunday the bishop announced that a new class would be started in Sunday school as of that day, and that Borga would lead it. "It will be," he said, "a class for advanced adults and will be conducted as a discussion of sources and kinds of information pertinent to the church. It will be open to all those adults who wish to attend."

The class met and Borga discussed in a general way what he had in mind. Then he announced that the topic for discussion next Sunday would be Joseph Smith's first vision.

18

At Borga's next class, he asked for someone to describe the first vision. A sister volunteered and read from the *Pearl of Great Price*: "I saw a pillar of light exactly over my head, above the brightness of the sun, which descended gradually until it fell upon me. It no sooner appeared than I found myself delivered from the enemy which held me bound. When the light rested upon me, I saw two personages (whose brightness and glory defy all description) standing above me in the air. One of them spake unto me, called me by name, and said, pointing to the other, 'This is my beloved Son. Hear him'."

"My object in going to inquire of the Lord was to know which of all the sects was right? That I might know which to join. No sooner, therefore, did I get possession of myself, so as to be able to speak, then I asked the personages who stood above me in the light which of all the sects was right, (for up to this time it had never entered into my heart that all were wrong) and which should I join.

"I was answered that I must join none of them, for they were all wrong, and the personage who addressed me said that all their creeds were an abomination in his sight; that those professors were all corrupt, they draw near to me with their lips, but their hearts are far from me; they teach for doctrine the commandments of men, having a form of godliness, but they deny the power thereof. He again forbade me to join with any of them; and many other things did he say unto me which I cannot write at this time."

Borga asked, "Was this account written at the time of the vision or later?" No one volunteered to answer, so Borga pointed out that the written account was made about twenty years after the time Joseph Smith reported having had the vision. One brother said,

"You mean, Joseph wrote it from memory after twenty years had passed?"

"So far as I can find," said Borga, "there is no officially approved written record other than what has been read to us this morning."

One sister remarked, "The members all knew about it. How did they get the information?"

"Does anyone have any answer to that question?" asked Borga.

There was no answer volunteered, so Borga continued. "Prior to the report, just read to us, the members knew about it so it must have been passed to the members by word of mouth. What are some of the outstanding thoughts expressed in this report of the first vision?"

One brother stated, "The Prophet saw God and Jesus Christ and talked with them."

Another brother volunteered, "This was an answer to Joseph's prayer seeking to know, of all the Christian sects which one he should join. He was told that none of them were correct. That he should join none of them."

"There is another account," remarked Borga, "in the Church library, of the first vision, but it is in a journal which has never been published. The account was written in the first person as if the Prophet had written it, but it may have been dictated by the Prophet to a scribe. It was written, according to the date in the journal, shortly after the vision occurred."

Borga read from the copy which he had made:

"A pillar of light above the brightness of the sun at noon day came down from above and rested upon me and I was filled with the Spirit of God and the Lord opened the heavens upon me and I saw the Lord and he spake unto me saying, 'Joseph, my Son, Thy sins are forgiven thee, go thy way, walk in my statutes and keep my commandments; behold I am the Lord of glory; I was crucified for the world, that all those who believe on my name have Eternal life....'"

He asked, "What difference do you observe between the published account of the first vision as reported twenty years after it occurred, and the one reported in the journal shortly after the vision occurred?"

Ethel volunteered to answer. "The report from the *Pearl of Great Price* states that two personages appeared and that one, presumably God, referred to the other as his Beloved Son, presumably referring to Jesus Christ. In the account referred to in the journal only one personage appeared, and he referred to himself as the Lord."

It was time to close the class and Borga announced that the next lesson would be a discussion of the Mormon concept of the godhead.

19

The following Sunday, Borga opened the class with a story. "A young man was riding in a carriage. As it crossed a bridge over a swift-moving stream he noticed a small child in the creek. He called to the driver to halt and jumped out of the carriage. He ran down the creek to a point below where the child was floating in the water, jumped in and rescued the infant, after which he returned it to its negligent but appreciative mother.

"This story has probably reminded you of something. I would like some of you to relate for us what it recalled to your mind."

A sister raised her hand. "My husband and I had taken our three children to the mountains on a picnic. Our youngest child, a son, was five years old and had not learned to swim yet. Our oldest child, a daughter, was twelve, and she was assigned the task of watching the young son to see that he did not get in the nearby river. The two older children got to playing, and I looked just in time to see my son slip into the river. I screamed and my husband ran, dived in and rescued him.'"

Another brother volunteered, "I was fishing in a river and observed a man approaching up stream on horseback. He seemed to be in a hurry. The river was quite wide and too swift. He apparently decided to swim his horse and to hang on to the horse's tail. As the horse approached the point where the river was swirling the man apparently lost his grip and was swept downstream. He apparently did not know how to swim. He was swept near to where I was, so I was able to pull him out. He seemed to be lifeless, so I gave him artificial respiration as best I could, but he did not recover."

Borga commented, "I'm quite certain that others of you could tell us of similar reactions to the story I related. I think, however, that the incidents referred to serve to illustrate the point I wanted to make, namely, that each one of us interprets, in a large measure, information that we received in terms of our own experience. Since we all have somewhat different experience it is not surprising that we interpret a given bit of information which we received in our own peculiar way.

"Likewise, individuals of different ages interpret a bit of information they get in different ways. If a father came home just before Christmas and told his wife and five-year-old son that he had seen Santa Claus in town, the interpretation of the father's remark would be interpreted differently by the mother than by the child."

Brother Dahl wanted to know, "Does this apply to the Mormon concept of God?"

Brother Morgan, of the high council, answered, "No this certainly does not apply to God. The concept of God is the same to all Mormons. It is constant. It is the same to a child as it is to the man when he grows up."

Another brother said, "If we agree with Brother Morgan that God is interpreted as being constant in character, and the same by all Mormons, I don't see how we can reconcile that with the Mormon concept of eternal progression in which God, as well as we, are continually in progressive change."

The time was up, so Borga dismissed the class.

Borga and Ethel were chatting after Sunday school adjourned when the bishop came up and asked Borga to see him after the others had left.

Ethel said, "Now what?"

"I think I know," answered Borga. "Would you mind waiting for a few moments?"

The bishop opened his remarks, "Brother Borga, I'm afraid we are in trouble. Your class has been such a success and has attracted so much attention. It has created quite a stir in the high council, and they have asked for a meeting with you, preferably one week from next Wednesday. In the light of this I think that we had better cancel the class for next Sunday."

"Did they give any specific reason?"

"I think that I had better let them answer that question."

Ethel was waiting anxiously, but all Borga could tell was that the meeting had been called and the next Sunday's class cancelled. But Borga had his own idea as to what would be discussed.

20

Borga met the bishop, his two counselors, and the high council. Brother Morgan, of the high council, was chairman of the meeting. He had attended several of Borga's discussions. He opened his remarks by complimenting Borga on his outstanding loyalty and support of the church since joining it; for the courage under great personal danger experienced in Missouri; and for his exemplar conduct as a member of the church.

Then he continued, "It was with some misgiving that we called this meeting with you. We recognize that you have a fine mind, but we feel that your thinking is somewhat disturbing to many of our people. We think that it is too advanced for them. Would you care to make any comment on this point?"

"No, I abide by the decision of you brothers. I have no desire to persuade anyone to agree with my thinking on these matters. I only desire to clarify my own thoughts, and if anyone can benefit by it, I will be happy."

Borga realized as soon as he made this statement that it was not exactly correct. He fully intended to try to convince Ethel, at least in part, to his way of thinking.

Brother Morgan followed, "Would you mind, Brother Borga, if we ask you a few questions?"

"Certainly not."

"Do you believe that Joseph Smith was a true Prophet of God and that he saw and talked with God?"

"As you know, I have supported that hypothesis ever since I joined the church. I call it a hypothesis because I see no way of getting verifiable evidence either for or against the account of the vision in which Joseph Smith is reported to have seen and talked with God. Also, I'm not sure that I understand what you mean by a 'true Prophet of God.' The account of the vision as given to us in *Pearl of Great Price* was not written until twenty years after it was said to have occurred. So, there is considerable possibility for error in memory on the part of Joseph Smith. Furthermore, it does not agree with the statement reported to have been made by him shortly after the reported time on which he had the vision."

Several of those present showed concern at the mention in the *Pearl of Great Price* is the only one I know anything about. Where is this other account to which you refer?"

Borga mentioned the journal in the church library, and pointed out that the report in the journal, made shortly after Smith is said to have had the vision, stated that he saw the Lord and talked with him. The account made twenty years later, as given in the *Pearl of Great Price* says that he saw two personages and that one spoke, referring to the other as his son. There are other differences in the two accounts also."

Brother Morgan said, "I would like to see what you think about another point. We believe that the framers of the Constitution of the United States were inspired by God. Are you in agreement with that?"

"So far as I can find from the literature, they were a group of individuals trying to solve a common problem. There were widely diverging opinions among them, but they all had the desire to arrive at the best collective opinion that they could individually support. I do not see that any superhuman had anything to do with their actions."

Brother Morgan continued: "Your thoughts seem very radical, Brother Borga. Do you have knowledge of the truthfulness of this church, and that it is the only true Christian church?"

"I have heard many members say that they have such knowledge, and I once said so myself. But my conscience has bothered me ever since because I had no such knowledge. It was plainly a lie on my part, for which I am sorry."

Some members of the high council were getting disturbed at Borga's answers.

"As you know, Brother Borga, we in this church hold that it is a sin to worship an idol. Do you agree with that?" asked Brother Stevens.

"It seems to me that it makes little or no difference whether the idol is real, such as carved in stone or cast in metal such as our angel Moroni—or is a painting on canvas—or is imaginary. If it helps the individual to interpret life, it serves a useful purpose. We know that man has imagined gods and goddesses ever since he started to record his thoughts about six thousand years ago. Since then all sorts of idols have been worshipped."

"Do you agree that God created man?"

"No, brethren, the preponderance of evidence, as I see it, indicates that the reverse is true. It seems that as man has developed, the more imaginative individuals have invented gods and goddesses. Maybe that's why we have so many kinds of gods recorded in history. It seems to me that man created god. It was a result of man's effort to explain and interpret life as he found it."

"Brother Borga, do you believe in God?"

"I have no evidence that he exists. Neither do I have any evidence that he does not exist. The hypothesis that he does exist may, and probably does, help many people to interpret nature and their lives. I, however, do not find the hypothesis helpful."

Brother Morgan turned red in the face. "Brother Borga, I think that you are headed straight to hell—in care of the devil."

Borga knew that this meeting brought to an end one phase of his life. He was certain that he could never return to leading an active life as a Mormon.

He knew that his relations with his father, Caleb Jones and with Jens Pedersen—all of whom had just returned from duty with the Mormon Battalion—would be strained. He was also aware that Ethel's father would strongly disapprove. Borga was very much in love with Ethel, but he was not sure what her reaction would be to a frank statement of his thoughts as he had expressed them at the meeting.

He knew that Ethel was anxious about the result of the meeting and he wanted to be the first to tell her. He had previously told her that he would contact her as soon as the meeting was over. He was well aware that she would be greatly disturbed by what had taken place. She had expressed joy and pride over the success as indicated by the interest and attendance at the Sunday school classes. He was afraid that she was not aware of the strong, adverse feeling that could develop among some of the more orthodox members. He knew that Ethel was very orthodox, but he also knew that she had a keen mind that was not closed to new ideas. He had hoped that she would appreciate his viewpoints, even though he was certain that they would disturb her.

She was waiting at her home and they left immediately for a walk so that they could discuss the results of the meeting and its consequences in private.

She listened patiently as he took her hand while they walked slowly around the Temple Square, and then up on the hill overlooking the city, where they could see the beginning of the new Mormon Temple to which Ethel had aspired to go when she and Borga got their endowments and would be married and sealed to each other for time and eternity.

Ethel said nothing as Borga explained what had taken place at the meeting, but when he was partly through, she began to weep, and by the time he had finished she was in uncontrolled grief.

In concluding his account, Borga said, "What hurts me most, Ethel, is that if we get married, I will not be able to satisfy what I know is your desire to go through those rituals for which you have strongly hoped. For this I'm profoundly sorry, but I have done what I think is honest and honorable."

The next morning, he described to his parents what had happened. His father was an orthodox man and had little sympathy with Borga's conclusions. His mother, who had never paid much attention to theology, but was persistent in teaching her children a strong code of ethics and morals, was more sympathetic.

He knew that if he had deceived his fellow members by leading them to think that he believed as they thought he should, when he actually did not, his mother would have been very disappointed and would have strongly disapproved. She was not happy with the turn of events regarding her son, but she took it in stride.

He felt the need for careful meditation, so the next morning he hitched up his team of horses and took provisions to stay two nights. His destination was the mountains to get a load of wood. In the surroundings of undisturbed nature, however, he felt that he could arrive at a more rational, objective and fairly definite conclusion as to what his next course of action should be.

On his way his mind kept oscillating between making plans for his immediate future and the sadness he had for the way in which the turn of events had made Ethel feel. He felt that she had endured enough already in her migration from Wales with her parents to Nauvoo, and then all the difficulties she had encountered in crossing the plains and mountains to come to Utah in order to join the Mormon church and worship as she wanted to.

He kept raising questions as to whether he had done the right thing by expressing his views as he had done. But he was always forced to the conclusion that he would have been a hypocrite to pretend that his thinking was other than what he had stated it to be. There just seemed to be no way that he could honestly change his viewpoints in the light of the information available.

He recognized that Ethel had seemed perfectly happy in her religious thinking. He concluded that it must be possible for individuals to concentrate their thoughts along certain theological lines with such intensity and faith that they arrive at a state of verisimilitude where they feel that they know that certain things are true, but which they nor anyone else can verify with facts. Therefore, in reality the ideas are based on faith alone.

After much struggling with his thoughts, he made the final decision that as soon as he returned to his home, he would make immediate plans to leave for Harvard University where he hoped to pursue his legal studies. He also decided that one of the first things he would do when he got back to his home was to make a visit to Ethel.

Borga told brother Evans that he had been considering for some time talking with him regarding his love for Ethel but recognized that there was a large hurdle that would have to be gotten over sooner or later. He could not quite bring himself to the point of discussing the matter previously.

Brother Evans took time discussing some matters, and then asked Borga to summarize his thoughts as expressed at the meeting.

"By studying and reading as widely as possible in the time available to me, and by giving a great deal of thought to the subject, it seems to me that from the dawn of history man made postulates about the unknown. In early mythology man has made postulates about gods and goddesses of various types—their functions, their relations to man, their effect on their environment, etc.; also, different religious developed postulates or theories about the unknown usually in terms of gods or spirits.

"Thus, I can see little or no difference between the basic motive behind theology and the motive behind mythology. This appears to be characteristic of all kinds of religions. They seem to all have resulted from efforts to satisfy man's desire to know the secrets of life."

Borga could see from the look on Ethel's father's face that he was very much disturbed at what Borga was saying, but he felt that he should continue.

"My plea is that every individual has to interpret such things in terms of their own experience and background. For the most part, it seems to me that most religions, and particularly Mormonism, do not permit this variation in conclusions from the accepted doctrine of the church."

Brother Evans listened to, what must have been to him, a painful discussion, then said, "I respect your opinion, but I do not understand it. It seems absolutely foreign to our way of thinking. Ethel's mother and I would be horrified to think of her marrying you under these conditions. A marriage outside the Temple would not be acceptable, and we are certain that any developing family relations would not hold in the next life. Therefore, we request that you not see Ethel again until she is feeling better."

"Thank you for your courtesy, Brother Evans," Borga said, and he walked away quickly.

21

The topic uppermost in Borga's mind, as he prepared to leave, he was unable to resolve. What should be his future relations with Ethel? His love for her seemed stronger than ever, but he was not certain that she could be happy married to him.

Indeed, he had considerable doubt as to whether she would consent to marriage under those conditions. In any case, he concluded that it would be better to let some time elapse before he discussed the subject with her, since they were both in a disturbed state of mind at present.

Three weeks had passed and Borga was ready to leave. He and Ethel had discussed their problems and there was obviously a strong bond between them. They decided to keep in touch with each other but made no commitments at present as to their future together.

The last Sunday evening before leaving, Borga went to church alone. He noticed Ethel standing by a young man whom Borga had not seen before. She beckoned for Borga to come over where she was and introduced him to a Brother James Snedden, a new convert to the church, who had just arrived from London. Borga was somewhat disturbed at his own reaction to this new member. He felt a distinct twinge of jealousy at seeing Ethel and the young man apparently enjoying a friendly conversation.

On Wednesday, Borga left for Cambridge, Massachusetts. He had spent much time studying legal publications, but he had no idea how well prepared he would be considered by the authorities at Harvard. Upon arrival there he had several discussions with officials at the University and was given several examinations, after which he was allowed to enter some advanced classes.

He buried himself in studies, except for two diversions in which he indulged. Ethel was always on his mind and he wrote to her frequently. His other diversion was getting acquainted with the local territory which was closely tied to the early development of the United States.

Some aspects of this country reminded him of his native Denmark. The difference between the New England area and the area around Salt Lake was remarkable. He tried to make every weekend count by going to visit such places as Bunker Hill, Plymouth Rock, Concord where "the shot was fired that was heard round the world," Lexington, and many other places. He crossed the Charles River often to visit historic spots in Boston.

Ethel's letters seemed to indicate that she had other interests and Borga felt so depressed that it began to interfere with his studies. He decided that he must do something to take his mind off the subject.

He joined a semi-social discussion group, on comparative religious and sociological questions. The group met once a week in the evenings and one of the professors in the field of sociology, history or religion led the discussion. In the group was a young Jewish girl attending college in the area. She seemed quite bright, affable and attractive.

Louella Newmark seemed to express herself well, and her opinions seemed to be recognized and appreciated by other members of the group. There seemed to be no difference in the attitude of any of the members toward her than to any other member.

Borga noticed that she asked many more questions than she expressed opinions which seemed to him to be appropriate for a girl of her age and training. Her questions were meaningful, as indicated by the fact that they were never ignored, and usually provoked considerable discussion. At the end of the discussions the group usually indulged in some refreshments, after which they gathered around the piano and participated in singing popular songs of the time. Borga noticed that Louella seemed very sociable on all these occasions and was always discreet in her behavior.

He and Louella became quite friendly, and after about two months of this congeniality he noticed a marked change in her attitude. She seemed quite depressed.

"Have I done anything to offend you, Louella?" Borga asked.

"No, Borga, it has nothing to do with anything you have said. It is some undesirable experience which I have had recently."

Louella had lived in a community where Jewish families were in the minority. During school her associations with her friends were normal and she had experienced no marked feeling that would indicate to her that she was not welcome in the company of the other students.

"Since my arrival in Cambridge," she said, "I have run into some difficulties. I planned and desired very much to join a social organization of girls and it looked as if I were going to be welcomed into the group. But when the final decision on invitations to new members was made, my name was left out without any explanation. I had to get the reason for this refusal through round-about inferences which gradually pointed to the fact I was excluded because I was of Jewish origin."

Ethel's letters had become rather cool and were quite infrequent, while Borga's friendship with Louella continued. Along toward Spring they recognized that they were quite in love with each other. Louella had discussed the matter with her family, and they were opposed to her considering marrying outside the Jewish faith.

Borga explained to her about his previous experience with Ethel and suggested that they give careful consideration to their relationships before going too far. They decided to take a trip to New York to visit her folks for a short time so that a mutual acquaintance could be made with her family.

Louella's grandparents on both sides of her family were Jews. She mentioned that this was the most orthodox of all the sects. They gave much attention to piety and devotion; their religion demanded that they pay strict attention to God's commandments; follow the Torah to the letter and abide by the words of the sages and the grand rabbis. The Torah was the written law comprising the word of God as given to Moses at Mr. Sinai. The Talmud, called the oral law because it was the compilation of the rabbinic literature deemed sacred. The Torah and the Talmud provided the rules by which the observant Jew conducted himself.

Louella explained that the men of this sect never shaved their faces, and at most social activities of this sect the sexes were rigorously separated. There was no social dancing or dating. The boys and girls attended separate classes. The women were seated separately from the men in the synagogue.

Her father and mother had broken away from the Hasidic sect because they had concluded that it was not suitable for life as they found it. They felt it isolated them from modern civilization. She said that this caused much unhappiness to her grandparents. But, she felt, that even the liberality of her parents tended to be too restrictive for modern life.

Borga thought that Louella's father seemed, more than any of the others, to be interested in getting acquainted with him, judging from the questions concerning the attitude of the Mormons toward the Jews. He was cautious not to offend him and explained that many Mormons felt strongly about urging other people to convert to the Mormons' way of thinking. Also, that the Mormons were taught to feel that this was an obligation which they should recognize since, according to the Mormon concept, it was the only way that these people could gain eternal salvation.

Borga assured Mr. Newmark that he did not feel that way himself and that he would be glad to give him an interpretation of the Mormon attitude regarding the Jews in as objective a manner as he could.

The Mormons looked forward to the reunion of the Jews in Jerusalem, as promised in the Scriptures. The descendants of the tribe of Judah accepted Christianity. The favorite sons of Jacob (Israel), Joseph and Benjamin, were promised that their descendants would be gathered from all parts of the earth. The Gentiles were considered by the Mormons to be all people who are not of the Mormon or Jewish faith.

The Mormon doctrine held that the descendants of the tribes of Joseph and Benjamin would be converted to the Mormon faith as they were gathered in Zion. The location of Zion was in America, the favorite of all nations, and Zion was synonymous with the headquarters of the Mormon church, which was considered to be the restored Christian church and would eventually cover the entire earth. Brigham Young thought of the Mormons as being Zion. Zion *is the pure at heart*, Borga told Mr. Newmark.

"The Mormons believe that the gathering of all three tribes will eventually occur and they will all recognize Christ as their leader. He will reappear not in Jerusalem, but where he began his work in the Garden of Eden, which the Mormon church holds, as declared by Joseph Smith, is in western Missouri, U.S.A."

Mr. Newmark listened politely and asked questions, but made few comments.

After a pleasant visit in New York, Borga returned to Boston. Louella stayed with her folks for a month longer.

He was a little apprehensive as to what attitude Louella would bring back to Boston when she returned from New York. Her parents did not commit themselves while he was there, but he judged that they were not enthusiastic. When Louella returned, he was prepared for a negative reaction.

He was not surprised; she was depressed. Her folks were much opposed to her marrying outside the Jewish faith, and she felt that she could not go against their wishes. The emotional strain was difficult for both of them. Since it was the second disappointment for Borga, he concluded that marriage was probably not in his future. He began to feel that religions might cause as much unhappiness to some as they gave satisfaction to others.

22

Ethel had never let the idea of marrying without her parents' consent enter her mind. It was just taken for granted. She had shown little interest in marrying anyone except Borga. Her father was so hostile to Borga now that it seemed unlikely that he would ever agree to Ethel marrying him. She was so distraught; marrying outside of the temple would seem like wasting her life. What hope could there be for her place in the celestial kingdom? She spent a miserable summer after Borga left.

James Snedden took a fancy to her and tried hard to interest her, but she could only offer him superficial encouragement. She was an unhappy girl. She threw herself into the various activities of the church with gusto, and spent much time studying at the church library. She loved singing, and one thing she liked about James Snedden was his voice. This brought them in social contact frequently.

Winter came early that year and caught most without their crops harvested and ill-prepared for the long winter. There was a shortage of food for the people and livestock. There was considerable suffering and death during the winter.

The Evans household had always been a pleasant one, even though the father had always required strict discipline. The difficulties between Borga and Ethel had, however, created a strained relationship. She thought each morning that she could stand it no longer. The days dragged. Each day, it seemed, was a contest between her and her father. Yet, it was not that her father was unfriendly. There were no harsh words spoken by either, but she felt that behind his façade was a firm, unbending will to refuse to consent to her marrying Borga.

Her heart ached for lack of her father's cooperation. This concerned her even more keenly because she knew that he had many other things on his mind, which the severe weather and lack of food and much sickness were causing in the community. Her mother was more sympathetic, but Ethel did not want to take advantage of the situation which might cause a strained relation between her parents.

Sophia, Ethel's younger sister, had always been a sickly child and now had taken a turn for the worse. As Ethel and her father watched by her bedside one evening, he said, "Maybe God has brought this upon us because of our wickedness. After obtaining a testimony as to the truthfulness of the Gospel, we should be able to conduct our lives better than we have."

Ethel did not want to dispute his statement. She sat there hurting inside because she knew that behind his words was a reprimand. If only she could give up the longing she obviously had for Borga, and accept the attention of James, a fine young man who would be able to take her to the Temple and be married in a way that God had commanded.

She tried with little success to get interested in James. She accepted a number of invitations from him to church activities. He had never been to Wales, and asked Ethel to tell him about that part of their country. She had made a diary and they got a map of Wales and spent several sessions discussing the subject, as Ethel traced her activities during her last summer in her native country.

She had lived in Worexham, Wales, all her life with her family, and had just turned fifteen. She was very happy because she had just gotten a job taking care of two children of Mr. and Mrs. Parsons. They were wealthy people with a home in London. Mr. Parsons had a number of business interests in Wales, one of which was the coal mine in Cardiff, South Wales. Ethel traveled with them during the summer. They paid all her expenses and she received a small amount of money. This opportunity gave her a way of improving herself by getting a partial education without it costing her much; something which she would be unable to do in any other way.

The Parsons were strict with their children, and with Ethel. They told her what she must do and how she must conduct herself as a servant to them, rather than as a member of their family.

Perhaps they wanted to make sure at the beginning of her employment that she did not make herself obnoxious. She tried diligently to do everything possible to please them, as she expected to get great benefit out of her associations.

Her parents were depressed regarding their economic position in life and their inability to change it. They were also dissatisfied with their spiritual life in the church in which they had been reared, and which Ethel had attended during her childhood. They had had some visits by the Mormon elders at their home, who explained the Mormon church's viewpoint on certain questions. Ethel's mother and father at that time were planning, if possible, to leave Wales the next spring. They, of course, would like to have Ethel go with them, and she was tentatively, at least, thinking about it. But she wanted to stay there during the entire year with the Parsons from whom she expected to get considerable benefit in preparing herself, no matter whether she stayed in Wales or went with her parents to the United States of America.

It would be difficult for them to get enough money ahead to make the trip, but the church would furnish some help for the emigrants.

Ethel had no opportunity as a child to travel much, even in her own little country of Wales, so she looked forward to her experiences that summer and the next winter in broadening her familiarity with her home country. The Parsons appeared to be well-educated. Mrs. Parsons was free in telling Ethel about the things that she thought Ethel should know. Ethel wanted to do everything she could to make Mrs. Parsons feel that she appreciated what was being done for her.

The first night of Ethel's employment, Mr. and Mrs. Parsons had a long discussion about their summer plans, and they had a number of maps on which they made certain notes. Ethel did not get much of the detail since she was not invited to this discussion and was careful to stay out of the way.

However, the next day Mrs. Parsons told her a little about the first part of their proposed trip which they would take shortly. She called attention to what she and Mr. Parsons had talked about the night before. They were wondering whether they should take the old coast road along the North Wales or whether they should take the modern road further inland. Ethel heard them laughing a little when they were talking about this.

The next day Mrs. Parsons pointed out that the Welsh in the early days used to rush down from their mountain strongholds and make raids on England. To do this they had to pass between the Severn River on the south and the Dee River on the north.

She told Ethel that one of the Saxon kings, named Offa of Mercia, got tired of the advantage which this gap afforded the Welsh attackers, and in the year 779 he forced the Welsh to build a great earth embankment one hundred miles long, cutting across this gap from one river to the other. She called attention to the fact that some of that dyke was still in existence. It was called Offa's Dyke, and Ethel had heard many times, people saying that they had crossed Offa's Dyke on their way to London, but she was unaware as to just what this meant.

The Parsons wanted to spend at least part of the summer acquainting their two daughters with the landscape, the people, the industries, and other features of Wales. Up north, they visited the old towns of St. Asaph, Rhuddlan, and Conway. They saw the beautiful Vale of Clwyd, said to be one of the most beautiful valleys in the whole of Britain. It was about eighteen miles long and seven miles wide. Mr. Parsons said that the valley was a productive agricultural area. He also pointed out that in early times the most powerful chieftains and richest monks lived in this area. They were said to be the guardians of the valley. The ruins of an old castle were still to be seen there. Conway and its marshy ground had a mournful significance in Welsh history, since it was the place where the conquest of Wales was finally signed in the Thirteenth Century.

They visited Ruthin, at the other end of the Vale. Mrs. Parsons thought that this town had considerable dignity and charm. They read the charter roles of the town and found them interesting, and funny in some cases. In 1295, these parchments said, "Wladusa, the laundress, was accused by one, Hugh Picot, and his wife Edith, of not returning Hugh's coat from the wash. Edith gave evidence that she had seen Wladusa wearing the coat with its distinguishing hood. Wladusa was able to prove that she had many years owned a coat with a hood, and therefore it was said that Edith was claimed to have made a false complaint.

"Things got mixed up in the laundry, apparently, even in those days," Ethel explained.

She remarked to James, "I will probably never be wealthy enough to send my laundry out, so I don't expect to ever experience such difficulties. So, you see, James, I shall always have something for which I can be thankful."

James was enjoying this session and wanted to continue with others. It was 11:00 o'clock, so he suggested that he would like to continue the discussions of Ethel's trip in Wales at their next meeting, and he hoped it would be soon.

The next Sunday after church, James requested the continuation. Ethel was of the opinion that this was just an excuse he was using, but she went along with it. They continued from where they left off the last time.

23

There were large numbers of people apparently wanting to participate in the meager fund set up by the Mormon church for emigrants to America, Ethel told James at the conclusion of her story about experiences in Wales.

"So now, James, you know how I spent my last year in Wales. We embarked on a ship on which were some emigrants from Denmark, and finally arrived at Nauvoo on the Mississippi River on the fourth of July, while the Mormons were celebrating that holiday. That is where I first met Borga."

"Do you ever long to go back to the old country, Ethel?"

"I haven't until recently. Now I sometimes wonder."

"Perhaps it's just a passing fancy, and I hope that our reviewing your experiences has not added to your unhappiness."

Ethel made no response, and James thought it best that he say goodnight. He knew what was troubling her and could think of nothing that he could say that would be helpful.

Caleb Jones had been a long-time confidante of Borga since Borga first arrived in America, although he was in total disagreement with Borga regarding the latter's interpretation of Mormon theology.

Caleb had also been a close friend of the Evans' family, and had watched with sympathetic interest the budding romance between Borga and Ethel. She had difficulty in communicating with her father since he had asked Borga not to see Ethel, following Borga's meeting with the High Council, so she turned to Caleb in her anxiety for advice.

After some preliminary remarks she came to the point. "Brother Jones, I'm very troubled over the feeling that exists between me and my father, whom I dearly love, but with whom I'm unable to communicate."

"I shall be happy, Ethel, to be of any help."

"You are aware of the difficulty between Borga and me." "Yes, I'm very sad about it. I cannot understand Borga's attitude regarding the church, but I can understand and sympathize with his love for you. I had hopes that you people would marry and play a strong part in upholding the Gospel."

With some difficulty Ethel continued, "Father asked Borga, before he left, not to visit me. He says that he is not willing to give his consent to my marrying outside the Temple. As you know, Borga could not get a recommendation from the bishop to marry in the Temple."

"Has your father made any alternative suggestions for action?"

"Not as such, but it has been quite evident that he would be happy to see me married to James Snedden."

"You have kept company with James to some extent since Borga left, have you not?"

"Yes, but I do not love him, and I cannot marry him. I'm so unhappy, life is a drag, although I have tried hard during the last few months to direct my attention to other things. I even tried to get interested in James, but to no avail.

"Borga and I have bound ourselves together, not by any formal engagement, but simply by our pure friendship and love for each other, which, it seems to me, a loving God would recognize. Is Borga's action such a sin against God that it is unforgivable?"

"I think not," answered Caleb. "Borga is a fine upright, moral young man. He has done much in support of the church. I cannot believe that God would intentionally condemn him for his honest interpretation of things as he sees them."

"I could never have realized," pined Ethel, "that such irresistible love between two people could cause so much unhappiness."

Just speaking with Caleb had given Ethel considerable relief. As she thanked him and prepared to leave, he suggested, "Time on occasion has a way of healing such troubles, Ethel. I shall make it a point to discuss it with your father, if you think that I should."

"I would appreciate it very much. But I beg your confidence since I should not like Father to know that I have come to you."

A few weeks later Ethel's father came home from the priesthood meeting in the evening. He announced with a note of rebuke that James Snedden was to be married soon.

This did not have the effect on his daughter that he thought. She breathed a little easier. Ethel had no desire to discuss the subject, so prepared to go to bed. But her father stopped her. "I have something else to tell you, my daughter. The man you have your heart set on—you must strive to forget."

Ethel was faint as she looked into her father's face. Her arms were hanging limp. "I would not set myself against it, if I did not think that it was for your good."

"Father, have you been so free from sin against God that you can judge Borga so harshly when he seeks only the truth?"

"God knows that I judge no man to be a worse sinner against Him than I am myself. But God forbid me from giving my daughter to a man who could not exalt her in the hereafter simply because I need His forgiveness for myself."

"Father," she said pleadingly, "surely you have not forgotten your youth so much that you know that it is hard to keep yourself from sin that results from strong love, and yet it is not even that grave a sin that Borga has committed. His sin, if sin it is, came about only through his striving for truth."

Brother Evans answered with an abrupt, "No!"

"Then there is something wrong with your memory," cried Ethel.

"You belittle the sin that Borga has committed much more than good judgment would justify. I will not wed my daughter to a man who has known the truth of the Gospel and has now abandoned it and, therefore, cannot enter the Kingdom of Heaven."

"It seems to me, Father, that a just and loving God would forgive such a sin as you feel Borga has incurred much sooner than many others."

Ethel was trembling with emotion as she cried, "If you are adamant in this stand, then I pray to God to end my existence here."

"I think it will do no good to discuss this matter further tonight," her father said. "You do not seem to see the light, my child, but I must persist in guiding you."

He wanted to say goodnight, but Ethel went sobbing to her bed. His wife and he stayed up for a while.

"I feel the need of some food," he said. Mrs. Evans got him some supper but arranged none for herself.

"You must stand by me, Jane, during this trouble. Ethel must get rid of her thoughts of this man."

"It could be more than she can bear," said her mother. "I'm not sure that you are right in this matter. It may be that God does not hold Borga's sin as great as you think. We are not all wise, you know."

"Yes, yes, I know. But we must hold to our principles."

Jane was vexed. "I think it unwise to set ourselves up in such strong opposition to our daughter. You must understand that she loves Borga intensely, and if you fail to yield you could be the cause of disastrous results."

"What are you driving at, Jane?"

"You must remember, Hugh, that many fathers have unknowingly met their sons-in-law."

His face turned angry. "Do you, her mother, have evidence of that sort?"

"Oh, no, I do not mean it the way you are concluding. But with such intense love as I have seen in this girl, who can tell what will happen?"

Hugh was angry. "How can you think of such a thing? God knows it is a dreadful enough sight for me to see her sorrow so much, but I'm sure that given time it will pass. I doubt that she will do anything rash."

"There was another man in your life that you would have married," he said, as he faced his wife. "How do you think it would have been if your father had yielded?"

Jane grew pale. "Who told you that?"

"Gronway Jenkins, long after we were married. But that does not matter. Answer my question. Do you think that your life would have been happier if your father would have given you to another man?"

Jane was now overcome with grief and could hardly speak. "That man did not even give me an invitation. He did not want me."

Hugh took hold of her hand. "So that is the cause of all of your sorrow during our married years. Is it not so, Jane?" She did not answer. He asked again, "Did you long for me to be like him when I could not? Was he always in your mind?"

"How can you accuse me of such things?" she cried. Hugh put his arms around her. She put her arms around his neck.

"Perhaps, Jane," he said, as he kissed her, "we have lived such a rigid, moral life it could be that we would be happier if we had more for which to repent."

After Borga's unsuccessful experience with Louella Newmark in Cambridge, he decided to make another attempt to get reconciliation with Ethel. He wrote to Caleb Jones, not knowing that Ethel had already sought Caleb's advice. The purpose of his letter was to ask Caleb to discuss the matter with Ethel's father.

Caleb went to the Evans' home and told them he had received the letter from Borga and was there to plead his case. Brother Evans asked Ethel's mother to join them, but she refused, saying, "If the answer must be no, then you must take full responsibility for our daughter's sorrows."

When they were alone Hugh said, "I fear for my daughter not being able to resist being led into Borga's ungodly way of thinking, because of her not having shown strong enough will."

"Brother Hugh," Caleb said, "you complain of her not having a strong will. It seems to me that she has shown a very strong will. You know, as I do, that she has had many suitors for her hand, both by polygamists as well as by unmarried men. She has resisted all of them. Borga is the only one for whom she has shown any real love, and a desire to marry."

"I'm well aware of that. But I believe Borga's will *will* predominate."

"I doubt it, Brother Hugh. Your daughter is like nearly all women with which I am acquainted. I have seldom seen one that was not able to rule herself and her husband as well. I'm well aware that your objection to Borga has not always existed, and is so now only because he sought the truth and came to a conclusion with which you and I do not agree, and which is contrary to the teachers of the church.

"But is it such a sin against God that it should be responsible for all this unhappiness of two such lovely people? Brother Hugh, I have known and loved these two young people, and feel that it would be a pity, and even a great sin, to separate their lives from each other."

Hugh got up and with some heat started pacing the floor. After a bit Caleb rose and took hold of Hugh's arm. "You are proud, Brother Hugh, but I urge you to reconsider your decision, lest these two fine young souls be damaged. You, in your pride, should raise the question as to whether you are stricter than God Himself."

Hugh continued to walk back and forth across the floor. Finally, he said, "So be it, and I pray to God that I have made the right decision."

24

Borga received a telegram from his father stating that his mother was very ill and suggesting that he come, if possible. He left immediately for the long trip back to Salt Lake City. He found his mother bedfast. Her physical strength was ebbing, although she was mentally alert. The pioneer life had taken its toll. Her heart was giving signs of weakness. "I'm so glad you are here, Borga," she said. "I have so many things to tell you and so many questions to ask."

"I'm happy that I could get here too, Mother, and I have many things to talk to you about. But for the time being, we must be cautious not to tire you out."

"Don't worry about that, Borga. Your presence is like a good dose of medicine."

Borga frequently conversed in German with his mother, which seemed to give her considerable pleasure.

Each morning his father held family prayers in his mother's room. After the prayer this morning his mother asked Borga to stop for just a short time as she had something she wanted to talk to him about. When the rest of the family had gone, she asked, "Are you happy with your theological points of view and thoughts now?"

"I am, Mother, but I have missed the pleasant associations of the Mormon people."

After a short pause, she said, "You know I would probably be happier about dying—and I think I'm going to die before long—if I felt as secure and as certain about where I was going and about what was going to happen to me. Your father seems to know exactly where he is going, whom he is going to meet, how they are going to act, and what the situation is going to be in the celestial life. This I do not know much about."

Borga changed the conversation to some other things in an effort to give his mother a chance to rest, but soon she began again.

"I observed a gradual change in your father's attitude after he joined the Mormon church. At first, he posed many questions and then gradually seemed to be convinced of the doctrines which the Mormons teach. He committed himself in public many times, although I felt that he was still a little uncertain. But after committing himself enough times he seemed to become convinced, and as the time passed, he became a staunch Mormon."

Borga attempted to find an excuse to leave because he was afraid of tiring her out, but she wanted to continue speaking in German. "I have always worked and helped others in the church through my membership in the Relief Society Sisters' Organization. I suppose, due to my inadequacy in expressing myself fluently in English, I have always refrained from committing myself in public about theological matters. This may be why I do not have such strong convictions as your father has.

"My marriage to your father was, of course, because I loved him; but my main purpose in life was being a good wife to him and a good mother to you children, and I decided that no religious matters would interfere with that. As you can realize, Borga, I have gone through quite an evolution, having been born and reared in the Catholic church, then marrying your father and becoming a Lutheran, and later your father and I having joined the Mormon church.

"I may have been too submissive regarding the theological matters. I have followed somewhat in line with your father's thinking without worrying too much about whether I was convinced of it or not; but all the time keeping in mind my main goal of being a good wife and mother."

Borga interrupted in an effort to let her rest. "In that you have certainly succeeded, Mother, and we adore you for it. Don't you think you had better take a little rest now?"

"One more thing, Borga. When your father began thinking about the Mormon church, I had some misgivings, but did not want to disturb him by my own feelings. Even after joining the church I had the strongest misgivings about permitting polygamy to enter into the lives of our family.

"However, I decided that my love for your father was strong enough that if he felt it was necessary in his religious life and really believed it, I would not object. Polygamy to him seemed a strong part of his faith, and gradually he was convinced of it. I was willing to abide by his decision."

One morning, shortly after Borga's arrival, his father asked him to say grace at the table. Borga had anticipated this, but he did not feel that he could pray in the same manner as his father did. It seemed unnatural for him to speak as if he were speaking to a personal God who was right in the room with him.

Reflecting his feelings, he started his prayer by simply expressing his gratitude and pleasure at being back with his family and friends, and at finding most of them in good health and spirits; and for the fine surroundings and plentiful food placed before them; and hoped that they all would continue to be blessed in this manner, and that his mother would regain her health, and that they would all be blessed with her presence among them for many years.

Carl, Borga's young brother, appeared to be intelligent, good looking, healthy, vigorous, and had fine manners. His moral standards seemed to be everything that one could wish for. They all expected that he would be called on a mission for the church as soon as he became old enough. Carl seemed to be following all the rules as given to the young people of the Mormon church. When Borga finished saying grace, Carl looked at him and said, "You pray differently than we do." Borga passed this off as easily as possible, knowing, of course, that his father and mother knew of his inner feelings and thoughts. Borga had not discussed such matters with Carl.

Christine began to lose her strength rapidly. Hedvig had arrived from Logan to be at her mother's side. The home was filled with members of the family. The neighbors, members of the ward, and especially the Relief Society Sisters, were all helpful. Members of the family took turns sitting with Christine because they did not want to leave her alone at any time in case she needed help. Borga's father had been at Christine's side almost continually since she had become bedfast. It was Borga's turn to sit with her through part of the night.

She had fallen into one of her short sleeps. As he started his vigil, Borga's father left to get some rest. As he sat there watching his mother, Borga seemed to live his whole life over again. He realized how much he was part of her, the inherited characteristics, of course, but they were not the things that impressed him at the moment. It was rather all the encouragement that she had given him to get an education; and most of all, it was those efforts of hers, in her quiet way, to have him develop into a son of whom she could be proud. This to her meant, above everything else, a person of high integrity, morals and ethics. Borga was touched with emotion as she awoke, but with some effort he held the tears back.

His father and the rest of the family were asleep. Christine was holding his hand, and while they were talking about various and sundry things she seemed to just fade out. Weak as she was, she made an effort to raise his hand. When he helped her, she got it to her lips, kissed it and then gasped.

Borga awakened his father, who was asleep in the next room. He got the rest of the family to his mother's bedside, but when he returned his mother had already died. Although it was 2:00 o'clock in the morning his Aunt Emma decided to get a message to the bishop. A Mormon bishop is on call night and day to members of his ward. He arrived soon after the message was put in his hands, and the president of the Relief Society came with him.

Bishop Harkness arranged the funeral accommodations with the undertaker, and with the help of the Relief Society made all arrangements for the family and saw to it that the funeral was carried out according to the wishes of the family.

Borga's Aunt Emma, his father's second wife, and the president of the Relief Society, Sister Carlson, decided jointly that they would undertake to assure themselves that Christine was laid out properly and that she was dressed in the proper garments, according to the ordinances of the church.

It was Friday morning and an announcement came out that the funeral would be held in the ward chapel the following Sunday, right after Sunday school at 12:30 P.M.

Christine's' body was brought home in a casket from the undertaker's parlor, and it was announced that she could be viewed there prior to the services in the ward chapel. Borga was surprised at seeing so many people with whom his father and mother had been associated for many years, and had now all come to honor his mother, and to view her in the casket, and express their condolence to the family.

As Borga greeted friends of the family, he observed Ethel Evans and her parents approaching. She seemed more beautiful than ever, and although he was depressed at the time because of his mother's death, the sight of Ethel sent a thrill through his system. He had not seen her since the rather sad and disagreeable experience just before leaving for the East, and their letters had gradually become rather cold and infrequent.

Borga had feared that the meeting would be somewhat embarrassing. Much to his pleasant surprise, however, the meeting was quite cordial, and he was delighted to shake hands with Ethel and her family, although he noted a coldness in Brother Evans' greetings, somewhat subdued by his formal politeness.

At the funeral, friends of the family including Jens Pedersen, Brother Jones, and Brother Evans acted as pall bearers. When the time came for the chapel services, the casket was moved to the chapel and placed just in front of the rostrum.

The chapel was filled, and an abundance of floral offerings adorned the casket. The choir sang the hymn *Though Deepening Trials* at the beginning of the services, and then the bishop called on one of his counselors to offer prayer, after which the choir sang the hymn *Oh, My Father!*

Bishop Harkness then spoke to the audience, expressing pleasure at having known Borga's father and mother and the family for many years. At the end of his speech he became quite emotional and it did not take long before many of the audience were in tears. Following his talk, a solo was sung by a baritone, *I*

Need Thee Every Hour, and then a speech was made by Jens Pedersen.

Never before had Borga heard Jens give a sermon—it was a homely one but his sincerity permeated throughout when he spoke of the family he had known a long time, and his close friendship with Borga's father while serving in two wars, and going through many hardships while working together aboard ship, and in California.

Borga was glad that his father had selected Brother Caleb Jones to give the main address. Brother Jones was the first Mormon that Borga had met after he came to the United States, and he had done much in guiding Borga in his first years with the church. He was a staunch member of the church and his speech expressed the ideas generally approved in the Mormon doctrine.

"The body must return to Mother Earth. Every person possessing the principle of eternal life should look upon his body as of the eternal earth. Our bodies must return to their mother earth. True, to most people it is a wretched thought that our spirits must, for a longer or shorter period, be separated from our bodies, and thousands and millions have been subject to this affliction throughout their lives. If they understood the design of this probation and the true principles of eternal life, it is but a small matter for the body to suffer and die.

"Our bodies are composed of visible, tangible matter, as you all understand; you also know that they are born into this world. They then begin to partake of the elements adapted to their organization and growth, increase to manhood, become old, decay, and pass again into the dust.

"What is commonly called death does not destroy the body, it only causes a separation of spirit and body. But the principle of life, inherent in the native elements, of which the body is composed, still continues with the particles of that body and causes it to decay, to dissolve itself into the elements of which it was composed, and all of which continues to have life. When the spirit given to man leaves the body, the tabernacle begins to de-compose. Is that death? No, death only separated the spirit and body, and a principle of life still operates in the untenanted tabernacle.

"It is a great cause of joy and rejoicing and comfort to his friends to know that a person has passed away in peace from this life and has secured to himself a glorious resurrection. The earth and the fullness of the earth and all that pertains to this earth in an earthly capacity is no comparison with the glory, joy and peace and happiness of the soul that departs in peace."

The services were closed by another hymn by the choir, *Abide With Me*, after which the Benediction was pronounced, and the casket was transferred to the white hearse. The funeral cortege then proceeded to the cemetery, and at the graveside a dedicatory prayer was offered by Brother Evans.

The ceremonies that day were the most difficult emotional experience that Borga had ever gone through. He marveled at the detailed confidence and certainty with which Brother Jones had expressed his concepts regarding life and death.

25

The first Sunday after the funeral, Borga met Ethel at church services. She invited him to have dinner with her folks at their home, which he gladly accepted. When he arrived, he found that the tension which existed at the time he left seemed to have largely faded away. Hugh was polite and friendly in a cold sort of way. They asked many questions about his experience at Harvard, and the vicinity of Boston. There was little discussion about matters in Salt Lake, except the activities of personal friends. Theological and religious matters were avoided until Ethel and Borga were alone.

He knew that Ethel wanted to bring up the subject, so he apologized for the difficulty which he had caused before leaving for the East. "I spent many sad hours thinking about it but felt that I could do little to rectify the situation. My conclusions about theology and religion have not changed to any extent. I was frustrated because I didn't want to disturb you and your parents. Yet you were continually on my mind."

"I, too, have been very unhappy," Ethel answered. "My interest in my religion has increased and I have read many theological books. I have also spent a great deal of time studying nature in general through reading of books in the church library. I now have a much better insight into the type of thinking that you have expressed."

Borga suggested, "Let's not discuss those matters further at the present time. Let us just enjoy each other's company."

He took every opportunity to be with Ethel during the next few weeks while he stayed in Salt Lake City. The world in some ways began to look bright to him again.

It was inevitable that he and she would get around to discussing theological problems before long. Ethel opened the discussion by stating that she would like to call his attention to a statement by the Prophet, Joseph Smith, when he was asked what the difference was between the Mormon faith and other Christian faiths.

He pointed out, "The most prominent difference is this: sectarians all are circumscribed by a peculiar creed which deprives them of the privilege of believing anything not contained therein. The Latter-Day Saints, on the contrary, have no creed but stand ready to believe all true principles that exist as they are manifested from time to time."

She also called Borga's attention to a statement made by Brigham Young. "I am not astonished that infidelity prevails to a great extent among the inhabitants of the earth, for the religious teachers of the people have advanced many ideas and notions for truths which are in opposition to, and contradict facts, demonstrated by science and which are generally understood. In these respects, we differ from the Christian world, for our religion will not clash with or contradict the facts of science in any particular.

"It seems quite evident from these quotations of our hardy Mormon leaders," said Ethel, "that they recognize the need for consideration of new facts as they are brought forth, and the continual re-evaluation of old ideas."

Borga listened without interruption to Ethel's discussion. "We obtain knowledge in several ways. One way is by our senses or empirically; such knowledge can be verified. This type of knowledge seems to predominate in your thinking.

"A second way is by intuition directly, and without requiring verification. This type of knowledge seems to predominate in my thoughts.

"We also obtain some knowledge indirectly by reasoning, but we must have some premise or starting point. For this we must often rely on one of the other ways of obtaining knowledge—that is, empirical or by intuition."

"Ethel, you've been getting into some complicated matters."

"I do not pretend to know much about mathematics," continued Ethel, "But I understand that self-evident facts lie at the base of this subject. As an example: the axiom that a straight line is the shortest distance between two points. This, I am informed, cannot be proven. We must take it as a self-evident fact.

"Or, as another example, how do I know that an experience, from listening to a large group of stringed instruments as they miraculously reincarnate the spirit of a composer, is beautiful. I can verify it to my own satisfaction and other can do the same, but we have to take it as self-evident fact that it is beautiful. We cannot prove it."

Borga was fascinated by the working of her mind. He could hardly realize that she had been digging into the literature, the way she apparently had been during his absence. She was definitely, he thought, striving to understand the world in which she found herself.

She next brought forth a copy of some Greek writings which she had found. Translated, the extract was from Phaedo by Plato. Socrates: "Such is the nature of the other world, and when the dead arrive at the place to which the genius of each severally guides them, first of all they have sentence passed upon them, as they have lived well and piously or not, and those who appear to have lived neither well nor ill go to the river Acheron, and embarking in any vessels which they may find are carried in them to the Lake, and there they dwell and are purified of their evil deeds, and having suffered the penalty of the wrongs which they have done to others they are absolved and receive the rewards of their good deeds, each of these according to their desserts. But those who appear to be incurable by reason of the greatness of their crimes, who have committed many and terrible deeds of sacrilege, murder, foul and violent, or the like, such are hurled into Tartarus, which is their suitable destiny and they never come out.

"Wherefore, Simmias seeing all these things what ought not we to do that we may obtain virtue and wisdom in this life? Fair is the prize and the hope great. A man of sense ought not to say, nor will I be very confident that the description that I have given of the soul and her mansions is exactly true, but I do say that inasmuch as the soul is shown to be immortal he may venture to think not improperly or unworthily that something of the kind is true."

Ethel commented, "It seems that even as wise a man as Socrates realized the need of some sort of picture as to what the future or the next life is, even though he could not prove it."

Borga took hold of both of Ethel's hands and said, "Ethel, darling, do you think you could be happy married to a man like me?"

"I couldn't be happy married to any other kind of a man."

"Well," said Borga, "let's get married sometime in the next three weeks, so that you can return with me to Cambridge."

They notified their families of their plans. Brother Caleb Jones was asked to perform the marriage ceremony. They asked permission of the bishop to hold the ceremony in the ward chapel on Saturday evening. The bishop agreed and announced on the Sunday prior to the ceremony that it would be held in the chapel. Dinner would be served by friends of the couple after the ceremony; and following dinner there would be a dance.

When Saturday arrived, Ethel and Borga were surprised to find such a large attendance at their wedding. Everything went off as planned. Ethel's father gave her away and seemed extremely buoyant, which was a little surprising to both Ethel and Borga.

Everyone at the dinner and dance seemed to be enjoying themselves. Brother Evans was extraordinarily happy and congenial, far beyond his normal mood. Ethel was a little disturbed, because she thought it not in line with his normal way of behavior. Everything seemed, however, to go well. There was much congratulating and well wishing. The whole procedure was started as usual by opening with a prayer, and at 11:30 o'clock, the dance was closed with a benediction, as was customary at all the proceedings.

Borga and Ethel left immediately for Cambridge, Massachusetts. Five days on their way they received some sad news from Ethel's mother. She had gone home with her husband and found that he had changed from his extreme buoyant mood at Ethel's wedding to a very depressed one. On the third day after Ethel's wedding, her mother found her father slumped in his chair unconscious. He had had a heart attack but recovered slowly.

They received the news while on their way and there was nothing they could do, except continue on their journey. They both realized that his finally yielding to their marriage was undoubtedly the indirect cause of his attack.

26

Shortly after Borga and Ethel left Salt Lake, members of the Danewel Group initiated a movement to establish a United Order, similar to what had been organized back in Missouri. Several other families were recruited who wanted to follow the idea set forth by Joseph Smith in the early days of the church. In all there were twenty families. All property was to be held in common. Caleb Jones was elected to lead the group, the church proposed him as bishop, and he was approved by the group. The area in which they owned property was organized as a ward of the church. Informally, the group, and the area in which they lived, was called Danewel Village. One strong, driving force in Caleb's mind was his conviction of the imminent returning of Christ to earth.

"There is no use of each of us trying to accumulate property on this earth," he argued. "We should cooperate wholeheartedly in helping each other to prepare for His coming."

At the beginning, separate sleeping quarters were built for each family; but there was a large, common dining room and kitchen. Everyone able to work was assigned tasks for which they seemed most fitted.

After a discussion with the members, Caleb announced: "We shall construct a large building to be known as the bishop's storehouse. All produce from the farms will be delivered there, as well as all surplus clothing and bedding made by the Sisters. Buildings will be established for specialized work, such as a flour mill, a slaughterhouse, and a machine shop. We will be as self-sufficient as possible.

"The production of every person will be turned in to the bishop's storehouse, and everyone in return may receive as his needs indicate."

There was some dissatisfaction, but in general it prospered, and soon developed into an attractive village. Everyone seemed to take pride in his work. Several of the men married more wives. This caused some dissension in the ward. Borga's father married Mary Andrews and, later in the same year, Jane Collins, both young women in their twenties. Caleb Jones also married two more wives—Sarah Jenkins, twenty-two years old, and Vinnie Nickels, twenty-one.

The United States government had sent agents of questionable types, at small salaries, to function in various capacities in Utah Territory. These salaries were supplemented by the agents in any way they could. An anti-polygamy law had been passed in Washington, D.C., and the persecution of the Mormons was building up. Detachments of the army were arriving. The reason given for the arrival of the military was to protect the telegraph line, which had been established, and the stagecoach line.

For some time, the Mormons had made no secret of the fact that polygamy was being practiced by its members. This was used as an excuse by their enemies for persecution, and as evidence of what their enemies called their debauchery.

Another reason for the opposition by the non-Members or Gentiles, as they were called, was the difficulty they had experienced when they tried to compete in business. The Mormons refused to patronize them. The Gentiles complained to the Mormon leaders, but were told, "We have no objection to you setting up business in this community, but we like to do business with our own people."

In the area where the United Order was practiced, Gentile businesses were non-existent. This was resented by the Gentiles.

In addition to the military and civil personnel from the United States government, there was a large migration of people moving through to California in search of gold. As was always the case in such migrations, there was a large percentage of unprincipled characters of both sexes playing their devious roles. Some of these people claimed to have been converted to the church, and made love to Mormon girls, both married and unmarried, and likewise some of the women married into polygamous families.

Some of these served as agents for unscrupulous attorneys seeking to get evidence to prosecute the Mormons.

Caleb Jones, in spite of his sagacity and high principles, seemed especially unfortunate in the selection of his wives. His first wife, Clara, was as staunch and loyal a loving wife as he could ask for. Her health had not been too good. She had raised two daughters and was now raising a child of his second wife, who had run away and left it. Its father was not known.

Later, Caleb married his third wife, Sarah. She was a devoutly religious girl—two years older than Caleb's oldest daughter, not too attractive—cared little about the way she looked and was somewhat careless about her housekeeping. Vinnie, his fourth wife, was one year younger than Sarah. She was very attractive, desired fine clothes, was haughty and had a nasty tongue.

There was great consternation about the anti-polygamy law, and the activity being taken by the government to enforce it. It looked as if all the polygamists would be taken into court. Some of them were taking their families to Canada, and some to Mexico, to avoid being arrested.

Caleb called his wives together to discuss the problem. "It looks as if all of us, with more than one wife, will be arrested and sentenced—if the government can prove that we are living with more than on wife. We are faced with a conflict between the laws of God in which we believe, and the laws of the United States government, some of which we think are unjust.

"In this conflict, the law of the government will probably prevail."

There was an anxious look on the faces of Clara, standing by the door, and Sarah, who was sitting in a rocker nursing her baby. Vinnie sat with a bit of a smirk on her pretty, but impudent face, looking out the window part of the time.

Clara was the first to speak. "Now this! After all that we have endured for the sake of our religion. What are we going to do? Everything seems to be falling to pieces."

Caleb answered, "As I see it, we have three options. One possibility would be to establish three homes—one here, one in Canada, and one in Mexico—and have one of you in each country."

Vinnie spoke with enthusiasm, "I like that. Do we get our choice?"

"You, Vinnie," said Clara, "have not been driven out of as many places as we old Mormons have."

"It sounds exciting to me. How soon would we go?"

"What other choices do we have?" asked Sarah.

"Another alternative," said Caleb, "would be for two of you to move to Canada or Mexico. Neither of these countries has laws against polygamy. One of you will stay here."

"Maybe that would be better," said Sarah.

With a forced laugh, Vinnie said, "That depends on what choices each of us has."

Sarah couldn't resist, "I suppose you would choose to stay here, where you can shop for pretty clothes in Gentile stores."

"Why not? Their stores are much nicer than ours."

"You pay too much attention to clothes. You would be better off if you would pay more attention to your church activities."

"Well, since you asked for it, Sarah, your rating could be raised if you kept your clothes in a little better condition."

"Well, at least I have a child, and I am caring for it, and that is more than you are doing to help in your husband's exaltation in the celestial kingdom."

"Maybe I could, if he would spend more time with me," snapped Vinnie.

"You know very well, Vinnie, that he spends more time with you than with me or Clara."

With a puckish grin, Vinnie said, "Well, you know it does take quite a little time."

By now Clara was weeping, Sarah's baby was crying, and Caleb was wondering whether the torture that he was going through on this earth was worth the exaltation which he expected in the celestial kingdom.

Sarah wanted to know, "What is the other alternative that we have, Caleb? You have mentioned only two."

"If your maiden names were not divulged, you could all claim that you are sisters. Which you are, in the gospel."

Vinnie got up, and with a bored look walked to the window. "Dear me, and mamma taught me that it was a sin to lie!"

"If that were the worst sin you ever committed, you would not have much to worry about," chided Sarah.

"Oh, for the love of heaven," shouted Caleb, "you wouldn't have to lie! All you would have to do would be to keep your mouths shut."

Sarah remarked, "Vinnie and I could probably get by as your daughters."

"In that case," remarked Vinnie, with a snicker, "you and your baby would be used as evidence to arrest Caleb on the charge of incest." Then, as if it were an after-thought, "Perhaps it would be easier in my case if I just ran away, like your second wife Jenny did."

Caleb had had enough. "We will have no more of this nonsense. I will decide in the next few days what course of action to take."

Sarah was not willing to give up. "If we in this family would not testify in court that we were your wives, do you think everyone in Danewel Village would do the same?"

Vinnie didn't wait for an answer by Caleb. "That's a laugh. There are several in the village who are non-polygamists, who ask why they have to be content with less of the common products from Danewel Village than the polygamists get."

Caleb said, "There are a few who are not willing to recognize the celestial glories as promised by the Prophet for those who are willing to live within the United Order. Jens Pederson, however, is not one of them, even though he is a non-polygamist. He has not taken up polygamy, but he is a staunch, loyal supporter of our movement."

Caleb started to walk toward the door as if the conversation were ended, but Vinnie couldn't resist making one more jab. "Sonja, Jens' wife, was too smart to let him," Caleb kept on walking.

Several strange men had been visiting the village without giving any reason for their presence. And about one week after Caleb's discussion with his wives, two of these men came to the door of Jens Pedersen. Sonja was home alone. As everyone knew, Sonja was strong physically as well as mentally; was not one to be pushed around, or to meekly submit to anything which she thought was wrong.

She had refused to let polygamy enter into her family for this reason, although she was loyal to the women who did practice polygamy. One of the strange men opened the door and walked in without knocking. Sonja was startled. "Who are you, and what do you want?"

We are officers of the United States government." He started to walk toward the door leading to another room.

"Have you a search warrant?" She was getting more angry every second.

"No, we haven't; we don't need one. We are looking for Caleb Jones. This is his place, isn't it?"

"That is none of your dirty business. Get out of here!"

The man picked up some papers from the table and started to look through them. This was too much for Sonja. She grabbed a broom handle which she had cut off for use when she stirred her boiling clothes, and for lifting the hot clothes out of the boiler during her laundry activities. With a healthy blow she whacked him over the head. He staggered to the door, which was open, and she gave him a shove. He tumbled down the steps to where his partner was waiting.

Just then Jens came up. He quickly sized up the situation and decided what had occurred.

"We are United States government officers," said the one who had waited outside.

"Have you a search warrant?" asked Jens.

"No, we don't need one. We are looking for Caleb Jones. Is that your name?"

"That is none of your damned business, and I will give you just three minutes to get off this property."

"We will, but we will be back."

As they left, Jens walked into the house. "Well, I see you took care of one of our visitors." Sonja did not answer. She was in such a rage.

Jens put his hat down on the table and wiped his brow. "Caleb has told me about his discussion with his wives. Do you know about it?"

"Heavens, yes! I think it is a mess, not only for the wives but probably for the children. They are being asked continually by other children why they have so many half brothers and sisters, and aunts, as they call the wives who are not their mothers. Also, about their many different grandparents."

Jens laughed. "You know, Sonja, I tried hard to explain to you the principles and the advantages of polygamy, but I never succeeded. You couldn't see the rewards to be obtained in the celestial life. I must admit, however, that you have kept me out of a lot of trouble in this life."

Sonja walked over to his chair and planted a healthy kiss on his stubbled cheek. "Well, I'm glad, Jens, that you appreciate small favors."

27

Under the pressure against the polygamy members of Danewel Village, the organization began to fall apart. Borga's father had asked for his son's thoughts on the problem in one of his letters and had been advised that where the church laws and the civil laws conflicted, it was almost certain the civil laws of the United States would prevail. Under these conditions, Borga thought that the only thing that his father could do, if he wished to keep his three wives and not go to prison, was to locate one in Canada, one in Mexico, and one in the United States. Borga Nielsen and Caleb decided to stay and fight as best they could.

Borga Nielsen was "called" to move his three wives and their families north to help settle Cache Valley, so was not in immediate trouble with the law. Caleb decided to stay in Danewel Village, near Salt Lake City, and fight his case in the courts.

Six weeks later, Caleb was hailed into court. He knew that his wives would be called as witnesses, and he was not sure just how they would perform under pressure.

Joseph Knowles, the judge, was hostile to the Mormons, and the jury was almost surely to be selected with the ideas of keeping out anyone sympathetic to the polygamists' viewpoint. Caleb could find no trained lawyer that he felt he could trust, so decided to act as his own defense attorney.

Mr. Buhler, the pseudo self-righteous prosecuting attorney, made his statement. "Gentlemen, we intend to convict, under the anti-polygamy law, every man now practicing plural marriage just as we already have done with a sizeable number.

"Our great and noble Nation cannot tolerate such a foul practice to exist in our midst. We cannot tolerate depraved men of dirty minds and bodies to degrade the misguided women of this Nation into a state where they are producing a generation of bastards.

"Some men have practiced this whoredom for years and are still taking their concubines. Many of the women you meet on the streets of this city fall in this class, and your children now are going to school and playing with children born out of wedlock. Do you intend to allow this degrading custom to continue?

"Today we lay before you the case of Caleb Jones."

Caleb arose. He had not intended to make a statement but changed his mind at the last minute. He looked at the jury. "Gentlemen, there is a slight bit of truth in what Mr. Buhler has said. Some of us have married more than one wife, according to what we hold is the law of God, which was not in conflict with any civil law until this anti-polygamy law was recently passed. We have loved and respected these wives. We have raised children by them. If you are unbiased, gentlemen, I think that you will find these children exhibit a very high order of morality. Also, you will recognize that they are well cared for.

"There was no house of prostitution in this city until the Gentiles came and established one. Neither were there any prostitutes on the streets, as there are now. Some in this courtroom, including Mr. Buhler, are undoubtedly familiar with that activity, even though his efforts at high-mindedness was an effort to lead you to think otherwise. Most of what Mr. Buhler said is an ungodly distortion of what is, in reality, a wholesome way of life." Caleb sat down.

"Call as first witness Clara Jones," announced Mr. Buhler. "Please state your name."

"Clara Jones."

"Are you married to Caleb Jones?"

"I am."

"Have you had any children by him?"

"I have two daughters."

"Are there any other women living with your husband?"

"Yes, he is married to two other women."

"Who are they?"

"Sarah Jones and Vinnie Jones."

"That will be all for this witness, unless Caleb Jones wishes to question her."

He looked at the jury with a sneer on his face. "No questions," said Caleb.

"Call Sarah Jones as next witness. Please state your name."

"Sarah Jones."

"How did you get the name Jones?"

"I married Caleb Jones."

"What was your maiden name?"

"Sarah Jenkins."

"Do you have any children?"

"Yes, I have one child."

"Do you realize that your child is a bastard?"

"No! No! He is an angel," cried Sarah, and was in uncontrollable grief immediately.

"I object to such cruel type of questioning," declared Caleb, almost in a state of rage himself.

"Objection sustained," said the judge.

"Witness dismissed," announced Buhler.

"Call next as witness, Vinnie Jones."

Vinnie took the stand with assurance and poise. Caleb was apprehensive. He was not sure what the nature of her evidence would be. He feared that it would not be good.

"State you name," said Buhler.

"You just called it. You seem to know it already."

"Your Honor, I request that the witness answer the question."

"The witness will answer, please," said the judge.

"Vinnie Jones."

"Are you married?"

"Yes. Caleb Jones is my husband."

"Do you realize that you are living in a life of whoredom?"

"You, Mister District Attorney, are an unprincipled scoundrel. You delight in getting a timid woman on the witness stand and crucifying her with your dirty innuendoes. You ask..."

Buhler was appealing to the judge to stop Vinnie, and the judge was pounding the table for order, but Vinnie continued. "You asked for the whole truth, but you try to eliminate that which you do not want. While you have had your dirty agents sneaking around honorable peoples' homes gathering information with which to prosecute them, I have been doing a little of my own investigation.

"We had no houses of prostitution in this town until you and your ilk came and established one, apparently for your depraved, vulgar convenience. Mr. Prosecuting Attorney and you Honorable Judge, have visited these depraved women yourselves, and if you want proof..."

The judge was getting nowhere with his pounding on the table, so he ordered the bailiff to remove the witness from the court-room.

The jury convicted Caleb, as he knew they would. He was imprisoned for a period, but not as long as he had expected.

Caleb was proud of his wives' performances and couldn't help but chuckle at Vinnie's spunk. She completely surprised him. He wondered how she got the evidence on the prosecuting attorney and the judge. When he had an opportunity to have a short interview with her before he was imprisoned, he asked, "How did you know that they had visited the house of prostitution?"

With a twinkle in her eye and a low voice she said, "I didn't, but I decided that if they tried to prove that I didn't, they would get themselves into a pretty bad mess. Now, if they don't strike what I said from the record, it will look bad in Washington for them either way. At any rate, I'm glad that I said what I did. If they decide to challenge my accusation, I may also end up in prison. But I'm not sure but what I can get evidence to substantiate what I said, and anyway, it was worth taking a chance."

28

After Borga and Ethel arrived in Cambridge, they spent their spare time visiting points of early American interest. When Borga was busy with his university work, Ethel spent hours in the libraries reviewing early history of the area.

They had two problems which gave them concern during the early part of their stay there. They were anxious to decide on a suitable way to teach their children—which they expected to have—regarding religion. Considering the difference which existed between them in interpreting theology, they finally decided that they would endeavor to point out the difference between those ideas which have been or can be verified and those which must, if accepted, be on the basis of faith alone. They recognized that this would not be easy and would have to be done gradually as the children developed capability of understanding.

The other question was where Borga would start his practice of law. Both Borga and Ethel had a longing to go back to Utah, but Borga knew that he would not be able to take an active part in church activities, although he wanted to support the church. He felt that it would be difficult to practice his profession under these conditions if he were to return to Salt Lake City.

He had noticed an advertisement by a university in Baltimore for an attorney to teach law there. The advertisement stated that the school was operated by a Christian sect, but that they did not require that their faculty members be a member of that particular Christian sect.

He filled out the application forms which at one point asked if he were Moslem, Christian or Jewish. He listed himself as a Christian.

Two weeks later he received a letter stating, "You are one of the two applicants which we are considering for the position, and we will be in further contact with you soon." At the bottom of the letter there was a postscript, which said, "Please let us know the Christian sect to which you belong."

Borga smiled when he read it and showed it to Ethel. At the same time, he showed her his answer which was, of course, that he belonged to the Mormon religion, When Ethel had finished reading it, Borga said, "I know what the answer will be."

He received a prompt reply. "We do not want any Mormons on our faculty."

Borga had become friendly with three other fellow law students at Harvard. At first neither of the four discussed religious matters, but as they became friendly and had begun to learn more of the background of each other, such questions inevitably came up for discussion. This friendship and respect for each other grew.

As the time came near for the completion of their work, they discussed the possibility of establishing a partnership office. They laughed about the uniqueness of their group. There was Ansel McCormick, a Catholic from Boston; Benjamin Cohen, a Jewish boy from New York City; George Bunder, a Baptist from Alabama; and Borga, a Mormon, from the "wild and wooly west."

They looked into the possible places to locate and finally decided that they would attempt to set up an office in Washington, D.C. Each had unique familiarity with certain areas of the United States, and they drew lots to establish the order in which their names would appear in the name of their new firm. The result was Cohen, McCormick, Borgasen, and Bunder.

The men and their wives met frequently in what they laughingly called "summit conferences." It turned out that all of the wives seemed to get along well together, and the meetings were largely social.

At one of these meetings, Ben Cohen said, "We have a unique group here in two ways, we came from different areas and we all have different religious ties."

"That is certainly true," agreed Ansel. "See if I have the story correct. You, Ben, emigrated from Russia and met your wife in

New York city where she had arrived with her parents from Belgium. You both belong to the Jewish faith. George, you and your wife are the only native-born Americans in our group, and you both belong to the Baptist faith. Both of you were born and raised in Alabama. Borga and Ethel belong to the Mormon faith. He emigrated to this country from Denmark and Ethel from Wales. And my wife and I both came from Ireland and settled in Boston."

"We have here what could be the beginning of an interesting and profitable international group," remarked Borga. "We have all witnessed strong disagreements and antagonism in communities because of religious differences, and some of us have experienced considerable persecution."

"Yes," said Ansel, "we Catholics got it in the neck in Boston."

"Well," remarked Ben, "we certainly were given a rough time in New York City."

"The Baptists have probably witnessed less difficulties than have those in the religions to which the rest of you belong. But we have had our troubles too. It seems queer that religions tend to split society into hostile groups. We are supposed to get much of our training in ethics and morals through our religions."

"What can we do in the teaching of our children to avoid this difficulty?" asked Ethel. "I would like to hear from some of you ladies."

Ethel had some definite notions on this point since she and Borga had many long discussions on the subject. "I think that we can teach our children, as they become old enough to understand, the recognition and distinction between those aspects of our religions, which are based on verifiable facts, from those which must be based on faith alone. I want to instruct my children—which I hope to have—in the Mormon religion, but I would like to have them learn about the religious experiences which their friends have who belong to other religions."

"I think that is an excellent idea," said Mrs. Cohen. "Why couldn't we have our children meet together, probably once a month. We could take turns explaining the concepts of each of our religions."

"That is a novel idea," remarked Mrs. McCormick, "and I would like to see us do it."

Mrs. Bunder said with enthusiasm, "I like the idea. Count me in."

These meetings turned out to be interesting social occasions. Since they were all young married couples, just getting started, they hoped to put this idea into practice as the children came along.

After some months, it was decided that it would be to the advantage of the firm of Cohen, McCormick, Borgasen, and Bunder if they would take turns making trips back to the areas from which they came, so that they could keep in touch with the various activities in their communities. This, they felt, would develop business for the firm. Since Borga had been away from his home longer than either of the others, and was the oldest member of the firm, it was decided that he should take the first trip.

29

Early in June, Borga purchased a team of horses and a Ludlow, a light wagon-type vehicle with a sturdy box frame on it, but with springs which made it fairly comfortable in which to ride. It was quite large and had a wooden framework over it which was almost high enough to permit an individual to stand up inside.

The wooden frame was covered with canvas. They built a cabinet for their clothes, one for food, and one for dishes and a folding table. A small kerosene stove was used for cooking and heating. It was crowded, but much more comfortable than they had experienced in their first crossing of the country. Their route was to follow the same trail as that followed by the Mormons as they migrated from New York to Utah.

Borga on several occasions had discussed his interest in Indian affairs with Ethel. This, he thought, would be of value in his legal profession. He hoped to develop his knowledge in this field during his visit out West. But shortly after getting started on their trip, he told her of his secret ambition that had been building up in his mind.

This was to be, as he called it, a side issue or a hobby. He wanted to develop some ideas to which he had given much thought concerning the various theologies of the religions of the world. He was impressed with the nature of their basic tenets, most of which, so far as his studies had indicated, had no verifiable information to justify them. They were, so far as he had been able to find, largely believed in so firmly by the saints of all religions that they were taken without question as representing the truth.

He hoped to contribute by investigating the facts as far as he could find them, relevant to this subject. He wanted to organize this information and present it in a book in which he proposed to develop the nature of the verisimilitude used in the religions of the world. Having been born in the Lutheran church, having a

Catholic mother, having been converted to the Mormon church while a very young man, and having had a love affair with a Jewish girl, supplemented by extensive study of the religions of the world, supplied him with a strong incentive.

Borga and Ethel wanted to take their time and enjoy the trip. Their first goal was Palmyra, New York. Here was located the grove on the Hill Cumorah, where Joseph Smith prayed for guidance and reported that he received a divine answer and had the ancient gold plates presented to him by God. Translated, the *Book of Mormon*, supplements the Bible in forming the basis of the Mormon faith.

They both recognized that being part of the Mormon migration they probably were biased in their views regarding the various controversies between the Mormons and other groups with whom they had had difficulties. They wanted to hear the other side of the stories as they visited the various towns and cities where the Mormons had lived, as well as places through which they had passed.

When they got to the various towns, they decided not to tell anyone that they were Mormons. They wanted to get all the information that they could, so they asked lots of questions, just as curious visitors. They were told many stories—some ridiculous, some amusing.

At Palmyra, after talking with several local citizens, they were referred to a former schoolmaster named Jim Tobin, who was supposed to be familiar with the local history of the Mormon activities. They introduced themselves just as visitors passing through and having heard something of the Mormon activity.

They had been told that he might inform them more completely. He seemed glad to oblige, and explained, "Yes, I knew old Joe Smith. He was quite a character. He was about seventeen years old in 1823, when he went out on that little hill over there (pointing in the direction of Hill Cumaroh) and prayed with remarkable results, judging from the stories he told about it.

"He was a very curious young man. He and I were not what you would call close friends, but he confided to me what happened in response to his prayer, and later wrote it down and it was printed."

Mr. Tobin displayed a printed report. They showed interest and asked permission to copy it, which he gladly gave them.

Ethel made a copy of the report. This account did not agree with what Borga and Ethel had been told in their Mormon doctrine. It was a copy of the account which Borga had found in an unpublished journal in the church library in Salt Lake City. They were surprised but tried not to let Mr. Tobin know. They recognized it as the account made, according to the date in the journal, shortly after the event was supposed to have occurred. Just as they were about to leave, he remarked, "Something rather queer just came to my attention. This is quite a different account which Smith made." He showed them a printed quotation which Joseph Smith had made in Nauvoo, Illinois, about twenty years later.

They looked it over and were familiar with it, but again they tried not to show their concern.

They noted that in the first account Joseph Smith was quoted as saying that he saw the Lord, whereas in the version officially recognized by the Church, with which they were familiar, he was quoted as saying that he saw two personages, indicating that one was God, whereas the other was God's son, Jesus Christ.

Mr. Tobin continued, "Not long after the first vision, Joseph Smith reported that an angel of the Lord presented him with the Golden Plates upon which were engraved in reformed Egyptian the account which he translated as the *Book of Mormon*. Joseph Smith claimed that he translated the story from the Golden Plates by means of a device called *Urim and Thummim*, which had been supplied by a heavenly messenger."

Their next goal was Kirtland, Ohio, where they saw the remainder of the Mormon activities, including the Temple which was built there. Up to this point on their trip, neither Borga nor Ethel had seen the territory previously. Here at Kirtland, Ohio, Borga had made his first contact with the Mormons after arriving in America, but Ethel had not seen it before.

It was here that Joseph first set up a complete and rather elaborate organization of the church. Converts arrived from the eastern and New England states.

The practice of adult baptism by immersion was established. The priesthood was organized, consisting of Aaronic and Melchizedek orders. These were open to all male members. The offices of deacon, teacher and priests were available to members of the Aaronic or lesser order, whereas offices of elder, seventy, and high priest were available in the Melchizedek or upper order.

The office of bishop was established to administer secular affairs, and a council of high priests to administer sacred offices. The entire priesthood consisted of lay members. No one was allowed payment for his services.

Sacrament service was provided, and elaborate missionary service was created which provided for a convert to become a proselyte for Mormonism.

As the new converts arrived, the city grew very fast. The arrival of Gentiles also swelled the population. Learning of Joseph's reputation to obtain revelations, many of the converts got so enamored with the idea that they began to report having revelations and claims of prophecy. Joseph could see that the situation was getting out of hand, so he frankly told them that only he had the gift of prophecy and of receiving revelations.

Borga and Ethel learned through discussion with persons in Kirtland about the Mormon history, that Joseph's claims that he was in direct communication with God concerning matters pertaining to the church was the greater factor which antagonized non-Mormons.

One of the local residents, Mr. Bole, with whom they talked, said, "The Mormons started a form of community ownership in Kirtland. The unsuccessful venture, along with the anti-Mormon feeling, which was building up, gave Joseph Smith great concern. He solved it in what came to be his usual way. He had a revelation, which he announced was the order of Enoch, the ancient model which the early Christians followed, and was the forerunner of the divine, heavenly society."

Mr. Cole, shuffling through some papers he had, showed them the following statement of Joseph's announcement of his revelation: "And with one heart and one mind, gather up your riches that ye may purchase an inheritance which shall hereafter be appointed to you, and it shall be called the New Jerusalem—a land of peace, a city of refuge—a place of safety for the saints of the most high God; and there shall be gathered unto it out of every nation under heaven; and it shall be the only people that shall not be at war with one another."

Mr. Cole remarked, "Joseph, in his attempt to carry this out, set up an arrangement whereby each convert arriving was urged to deposit his money with the bishop, with the provision that the convert be given land in return. This represented their inheritance in the New Jerusalem. This form of communism did not work well, and led to considerable difficulties, which added to the antagonism by the non-Mormons."

"Well, what happened then?" asked Borga.

Mr. Cole continued, "Joseph Smith was not easily daunted. He had another revelation. The church established the Order of Enoch in a sparsely settled area of Missouri. Here would be founded the New Jerusalem, the City of the Saints."

"Did the Mormons move from Kirtland to Missouri?" asked Ethel.

"Yes, but that is a long, bloody story. You should get some of the literature on it. There is plenty of it written by non-Mormons as well as by Mormons."

"What happened to the Temple?" asked Ethel.

"It's still there. You can see it." He pointed in the direction of the Temple.

"The Mormons lost control of it in the financial crisis and resulting dissension among the members. Now it is owned by a splinter group called the *Reorganized Church*."

Borga and Ethel recognized this group as the church which made Joseph' and Emma's oldest son, Joseph, Junior, its leader. "It is called the *Reorganized Church of Jesus Christ of Latter-Day Saints*," Mr. Cole said.

Without doubt, as far as Ethel and Borga could tell, both of what they were hearing on this trip and from Borga's memory, the Mormons at Kirtland had been riddled by apostasy—and the debacle had been consummated by financial chaos.

Borga and Ethel moved on from Kirtland to Missouri where they visited De Witt, Far West and Adam-ondi-Ahman, the latter place pronounced by Joseph Smith as the site of the Garden of Eden. Borga had visited all these places and had many memorable but some very undesirable experiences. Ethel had never seen them before.

The inhabitants of Missouri were of a different background from the New Englanders and Westerners who had settled Kirtland. The Missourians were more of a hard, pioneer type. They were strongly in favor of slavery. The Mormon church had announced that Negroes were welcome to join the church. In fact, several had already done so. There was a restriction, however, that they could not hold the priesthood, but this did not seem to attract much attention. The Mormon opposition to slavery was a source of irritation to the Missourians.

Many of the persons from Kirtland who settled in this area of Missouri were apostates of the Mormon church. Some of them had acquired large holdings of the better lands before the main body of Mormons arrived.

Sidney Rigdon, a close associate of Joseph, and a strong proponent for the community-type ownership for property, upon his arrival in Missouri was deeply depressed over the failures at Kirtland. He put much of the blame on the apostates and, in fact, had deep resentment against them. He felt strongly that a communist type of economy should be set up among the Mormons. Word of this proposal spread among the Missourians, and this stirred up further resentment against the Mormons.

It was here that some claiming membership in the Mormon church had established a secret military organization called the *Sons of Dan* or *Danites*.

Rigdon had made a speech at Far West in which he revealed his hostile feelings against the enemies of the church. This speech was intense and passionate, and near the end he explained, "If the country cannot be freed of these men in any other way, I will assist in trampling them down, or erect a gallows on the square of Far West, and hang them."

This speech created more ill will for the Mormons. Knowing this background, Borga and Ethel wanted to get some local feeling regarding the Mormons. Their inquiries led them to a Mr. Moore, of Gallatin, who had an account of some of the early history of Davies County. He was willing to help them, and not only allowed them to review the report, but was willing for them to copy it. It was captioned, "The War with Mormons in Missouri," by Henry Billings.

"The Mormons started out to capture the state of Missouri. So confident were they of their ability to do so, that Joseph Smith, their Prophet and Leader, issued his proclamations ordering the insurrection, and declaring in that proclamation that he would eat Christmas dinner in St. Louis. The citizens of the county were aware that trouble was brewing, and parties were constantly scouring the country watching the actions of the Mormons. One evening, a party of sixteen men, who had been watching the road leading to Diamon in this county, came to Gallatin and reported that they had been chased by a troop of Mormons.

"Jacob Willis, who was one of the party, stopped over night with James Worth, who lived northeast of town on the ridge. The balance of us occupied the back room of Billings' store. There was not much sleeping done. The Mormons had run David Smith pretty close, and he declared that they had shouted to him they would have Gallatin by the rising of the next morning's sun. The boys laughed at him, and told him that it was only imagination, that he was so frightened he did not know what he heard; but whether they believed him or not they were all up and had their horses hitched to their rack by daylight.

"When I went down to my breakfast the boys told me to tell Willis to hurry up; they were waiting for him. I had scarcely reached Worth when I heard the boys hollering. I supposed they were calling for Willis, and so told him. We soon heard the clattering of horses' feet and looking out we saw our boys coming up under the whip with one hundred fifty Mormons close in their rear.

"The Mormons stopped when they reached the house. Surrounding it, they took Worth and myself prisoners. They brought us up town and kept us about two hours, then told us to 'git,' and we obeyed orders. In the meantime, they were sacking Smithers' store and other houses in the town.

"As soon as the Mormons had possession of Gallatin, they commenced sacking the few houses in the place. My tailor shop was short work—they got the $144 worth of clothes belonging to my customers—and all my clothes, excepting what I had on, even taking my hat as I was wearing an old-fashioned knit cap.

"The old man Pierce was living in a log house. They gave him permission to move his goods, which he did the same day. There was another house north of the square but not occupied. These, with my shop and Smithers' storehouse, were the only houses in town fit to use.

"Smithers' store was a big haul for them. It was a regular country store on a large scale. They sent back to Diamon for teams to haul the goods away.

"No country store was complete without a good supply of whiskey, brandy and wine, and Smithers had plenty of these articles on hand. It was amusing to see how often the Mormons sampled the goods.

"Before they turned us loose, two-thirds of them were drunk, but they got all the goods out before they burned the house. This was the fate of all the houses. They also burned the residences of Norman Snell and James Worth, who lived just outside the town.

"There were two other log yards in town with no roofs on them. The Mormons left them standing. As soon as the war was over, these two were roofed and turned into business houses, one as a saloon and the other as a storehouse.

"At the time Gallatin was burned, my father lived three miles south of Winston, on the Marrow Bone Creek, and when Worth and I were turned loose he harnessed his mare to his one-horse wagon, put his wife and children into it and started for father's, he and I footing it through six inches of snow. We had to travel fully fifteen miles and did not reach our destination until after dark. The next morning Worth and family continued their way to Richmond in Ray County.

"The Mormons promised Worth that he could have his household goods if he would send after them the next day, and that they would not burn his house until he got his goods away. Worth hired father to go to Gallatin after them. The arrangements were made that night. Father was to start early on horseback and have the goods already to load when James Winter and I got there with the wagon and oxen. Oxen travel slowly, and it was considerably past noon when we reached the place where Gallatin had been.

"We met father on the way who told us to turn back. While he was packing Worth's goods, another band of Mormons came upon him and advised him if he valued his health, he'd better leave those goods alone and vacate the premises—that the atmosphere was unhealthy.

"The road from Gallatin intersected the Mormon Trail from Davies County to Far West, in Caldwell County. After getting onto that trail we had to follow it about six miles to the crossing of Dog Creek; it was dark before we struck the Mormon Trail.

"When we got out about the head of Honey Creek, father suggested that it would be well for him to go ahead and have the feed ready for the oxen, and supper for us when we got there.

"He had been gone about a half an hour when we heard the clatter of horses' feet coming toward us and I said to James, 'It's father with someone after him.' When they came to the wagon father stopped, but the four men went on, probably thinking the wagon was loaded. Every little while we would suggest to father that he had better go on ahead and have supper prepared for us. But he stayed with us until within a half of a mile of the home.

"It was about two miles from father's to where the Mormon Trail crossed Marrow Bone Creek, and as it was entirely a Mormon settlement, we got all the news. They did not try to keep secret what they were doing or intended doing. They had no doubt as to their capturing the whole state of Missouri.

"For over two weeks we could stand in our dooryard of a night and cabins burning; scarcely one was left standing in the county, unless occupied by Mormons."

30

While Ethel was making a copy of the account which Mr. Moore had presented, Borga continued the discussion with him. Mr. Moore remarked that the Missourians wanted to have slavery, and the Mormons did not approve of it. This difference, he felt, caused much of the trouble. He said, "Although the Mormons did not approve of slavery, they certainly held a curse over the Negroes."

He went for proof of his statement and returned, much to Borga's surprise, with a *Book of Mormon*, and called his attention to the following quotation: "wherefore, as they were white and exceedingly fair and delightsome that they might not be enticing to my people, the Lord God did cause a skin of blackness to come upon them."

He explained to Borga and Ethel, "The Mormons did allow Negroes to become members of the church, but the Negroes were not allowed to hold the priesthood, and the curse was permanent on the Negroes.

"The Mormons took a little less severe attitude regarding the American Indians, whom they called Lamanites, since their skin was only brown."

To confirm this, he referred to another quotation in the *Book of Mormon*. "And the skins of the Lamanites were dark, according to the mark which was set upon their fathers which was a curse upon them because of their transgression and their rebellion against their brethren..."

Then he turned to another point and read, "...for this people shall be scattered, and shall be dark, a filthy and loathsome people beyond the description of that whichever hath been amongst us..."

Mr. Moore told them, "The Mormons held that the Negroes, because of the extreme curse that had been placed upon them with their black skin, could never be relieved of it; but the Indians by repentance and proper living could eventually improve their lot."

To prove this, he turned to another page in the *Book of Mormon*: "and many generations shall not pass away among them ere they shall be white and delightsome people."

These things were, of course, familiar to Borga and Ethel, but they thanked Mr. Moore for the information with which he had provided them.

They tried to patch together the information, which they had known from their Mormon heritage, and that which they had recently heard from various people with whom they talked in Missouri. It was certain, they concluded, that there was fault on both sides, but there was little doubt that the local element in Missouri at the time the Mormons were there, as judged even by non-Mormon references, had a high percentage of ruffian pioneers. They were not recognized as prone to brotherly love, especially if it interfered with their personal activities.

Borga and Ethel found nothing physical, such as houses or anything of that sort, that was reminiscent of a Mormon activity in any of the places they visited in Missouri; but it was nevertheless extremely interesting to visit these areas over which Borga had traveled and had had many experiences but which Ethel had not seen, and yet both had discussed many times in connection with their Mormon studies.

Borga was especially anxious to see Far West. It was here that Caleb, Jens and he had returned, under instruction of Brigham Young, to help lay the cornerstone of the temple which Joseph Smith had envisioned for that area. Brigham Young felt that to carry out the act of laying the cornerstone would give a boost to the morale of the Mormons. Borga, however, could find no trace of their efforts...

The next point on their travel was Nauvoo, Illinois. This was probably the high point of their trip since this was where they had first met when Ethel arrived on the *Maid of Iowa* from Wales.

They had anticipated considerable pleasure in Nauvoo because of their having first met there, but they were sadly disappointed by the pathetic sight as they observed the destruction and deterioration that had taken place since they left.

From several discussions with local citizens of Nauvoo, they got the same general opinion as expressed by Mrs. George, who seemed to be an intelligent woman with definite opinions.

"We did not like them for several reasons," she said speaking of the Mormons. "One, was their practice of polygamy; and they tried to combine church and state. We did not like their theology, and we didn't like the way they stole the secret rituals of the Masonic Lodge and adapted them to their secret practice, in what they called their endowment rituals in their Temple."

The temple on which the Mormons had spent so much effort, and on which Borga himself had spent many days, was a disheartening sight of destruction.

They visited Carthage, only a short distance from Nauvoo, and saw the jail where Joseph Smith and his brother Hiram were murdered by the drunken mob.

One local resident, Mr. James, with whom they talked, said, "Governor Ford had arrested Joseph Smith, his brother Hiram, Willard Richards and John Taylor and placed them in the Carthage jail for their own protection. Willard Richards was allowed to go in and out of the prison. The militiamen were all hostile, but the group from Warsaw had been whipped into a frenzy by the local paper, the *Warsaw Signal*, Governor Ford, recognizing this, had sent the unit home before he left. However, they went only a short distance and then returned. He had left what was called Carthage Greys of the Militia to guard the prisoners.

"Joseph Smith had smuggled an order out with Richards for Jonathan Dunham, in charge of the Mormon Legion. It never arrived. If it had, there would have been hell to pay and a bloody battle, which might have had grave consequences. A group of militiamen, with blackened faces, broke into the prison and shot Joseph Smith, Hiram Smith and John Taylor."

As Borga and Ethel rode west from Nauvoo, almost every hill, river and valley reminded them of some of the experiences which they had realized with the Mormon migration west.

After crossing the Mississippi River, they drove north to Iowa City, which was the town in America where the Mormon handcart pioneers had arrived from Europe, and had started their pulling or pushing of their handcarts from there on to Salt Lake.

Borga and Ethel were directed by an old man to some old shops where he said, "The Mormons built their handcarts, which they used on their migration to Salt Lake."

From there, they followed the old Mormon Trail through Iowa to Winter Quarters, which by then had been called Omaha. Here they both had many experiences recalled. They had spent a winter there with the first group of Mormons.

They went down to the old cemetery where they had witnessed the burial of many people whom they had known, and many of them were close friends. There had been much suffering and death during that first year in Winter Quarters. This was the only remaining physical evidence of the Mormons having been there. They found no one who could give them any further information.

From that point on to Salt Lake City—as they moved along—they called attention to each other of the various experiences and memories about the terrain over which they passed.

They were amazed as they were reminded of the differences between the reports which they as Mormons were acquainted with, and those they were told about along the way by non-Mormons. They recognized that the real situation probably rested somewhere in between the two versions.

Ethel said, "You know, Borga, I spent much time in the church library at Salt Lake City, but it seems queer that I did not find some of the stories and items to which our attention has been called on this trip. I was not allowed in one particular room in the library, the reason for which I do not know."

31

As Borga and Ethel approached Salt Lake City from around the north end of the lake, with the Wasatch Mountains on the east and the Salt Lake on their west, Ethel's heart quickened as she anticipated meeting her parents. These feelings were alternated with surges of pang when she thought of the possible reaction of her father.

"Borga, I fear the possibility of a cold or even hostile attitude that my father might exhibit toward us. Quite possibly he put on a gay front at our wedding. There are grounds for fear as indicated by his heart attack shortly after the wedding. I'm not at all certain what his attitude is since his recovery. Mother's letters were somewhat evasive and devoid of information on this point."

Ethel was prepared to receive some pang when she arrived at her old home, and to observe the situation with her parents emotionally as well as physically, and compare it with what might have been if she had followed her father's advice.

As they approached the city, they were awed by the fantastic growth which had taken place, especially the Temple and other church buildings. They drove down south Main Street to Ethel's own home. Her mother and father met them with much cordiality and made them welcome.

Ethel could see, however, that it would be a delicate matter for Borga and her father to remain together for long. Fortunately for Ethel, Borga wanted to spend most of his time out in the surrounding Indian Territory, studying their situation

After a few days visiting relatives and friends in the city, Borga went on to his studies and left Ethel for a leisurely visit with her parents and friends. His relatives had moved to Cache Valley, about one hundred miles to the north, and Borga and Ethel expected to visit them before returning to Washington, D.C.

She found her visit with her parents and friends pleasant. She took every opportunity to attend church services. She had missed this pleasure while in Cambridge and in Washington. But when she privately asked herself, "Was it the religious influence that I missed, or was it the social contact with close friends?" She was not certain of the answer.

Some of her friends who knew the background of her and Borga asked questions about their religious life in the east, to which Ethel adroitly gave answers. The religious background of the members of Borga's law firm was always an interesting topic of conversation.

One of her friends commented, "I can't imagine a Catholic, a Jew, a Baptist, and a Mormon working together harmoniously."

Ethel noticed that all her friends seemed to admire Borga, and this, of course, pleased her. In her spare moments she wondered what information he was getting. She knew of his scrupulous honesty. If he did not approve of what he found, his reasons had ceased to be any mystery to her. They were the very roots of his nature—the bones and tissue of his make-up. She knew that he would see and hear things with which he would disagree, and she hoped that they could complete their visit without any outward conflict between her father and her husband.

Borga was prodigiously busy in his desire to get as well informed as possible. His letters indicated that he was losing no opportunity to discuss problems, not only with the Indians themselves, but also with the Indian agents and the people with whom the Indians came in contact. Many of whom were Mormons.

He was accustomed to his being well received in groups, which she attributed to his appreciative manner. However, she thought sometimes that a little more subdued reaction might be better. He reacted in a light and somewhat jovial mood, even when he disagreed somewhat, as if he were taking part in a game. Anger seldom, if ever, showed in his reactions.

He finally returned from his trips through the Indian Territory. "Our legal organization in Washington can be of great help to the

Indians in seeing that they got justice, at least in part. We made friends with many of the Indians.

"I intend to make a careful study of the contracts which the various government agencies have made with them, and expect to put the results of this investigation into practice in obtaining justice for them."

They had to start on their return trip soon, so he was busy getting things in order. Hugh Evans showed no indication of interest in the results of Borga's trip. He asked no questions regarding his impressions, although he was always formally polite.

There was little time for Ethel to interrogate her husband, but she knew that there would be plenty of time during the long trip back to Washington. She vowed that once she was seated beside him in the Ludlow, she would ask plenty of questions. His trip was mainly to gather information relative to the Indians, but she was quite certain that he would keep his eye open for information which he could use in his studies of religions, and she was more interested in the latter than she was in the affairs of the Indians. No reference to the book was discussed with her folks, or anyone else in Salt Lake City.

They drove north to Logan from Salt Lake City and entered Cache Valley, following Box Elder Creek into Mantua Valley and then over the Divide, where they could look down on the beautiful Cache Valley floor. They were much impressed and delighted at the first sight of this area. Cache Valley had an almost level floor extending north and south and surrounded by rugged mountains. The valley itself was about five to twelve miles in width, and about fifteen miles long. Hedvig had told them in some of her letters how the Swiss people who had joined the Mormon church, and had come into Cache Valley, were delighted with it because it reminded them so much of their native country.

Borga had left the first contingent of Mormons while they were on Green River, under instructions to explore the valley which had been briefly described by some trappers. He had approached the valley from the east on horseback with two companions, riding southward to meet the remainder of the Saints in what was later named Salt Lake City. Borga thought that the valley was beautiful then, and he was still favorably impressed with it.

The floor of the valley was about 4,600 feet above sea level. The range of mountains on the west was much lower than those on the east. The mountains on the east were rugged, with some of them running up to heights of approximately 10,000 feet.

Borga's father had been "called" to help settle Cache Valley. He had built a new home, which was located at the corner of second east and third north. The Mormons always laid their town out, "square with the world," as they said. The streets ran east and west, north and south, in many cases with disregard for hills.

His father decided for the time being to try to keep his three wives together. They each had their own bedroom, but the remainder of the house was communal. It was an enjoyable occasion, especially for Borga, to be with his family. He found it a bit strange, however, getting used to seeing all the strange noses on his young half-brothers and sisters. He noted that no children had been born since the new law against polygamy had been passed.

Borga was happy to see his sister Hedvig, and Jens' adopted son Gustaf, living a normal, contented life after passing through several unhappy years. For two years before Gustaf was "called" on his mission, he and Hedvig had been in love. Just before he was to leave, their affection for each other had led them too far. The prospective missionaries were always interrogated to determine their fitness to undertake missionary activities. They were carefully questioned as to their morality. When Gustaf was being interrogated, however, he did not admit his guilt.

The truth caught up with him four months after he had left on his mission. Hedvig realized that she was pregnant. He was asked by the authorities to return. They were married but not in the Temple, as they both had wished, since neither could expect to receive a recommendation from their bishop. They loved each other but were remorseful and felt guilty and uncomfortable among their former friends in Salt Lake City. They decided to move to Logan and start life anew. They worked diligently in the church and by the time Borga and Ethel arrived they had behaved so well that the bishop had given them recommendations, and they had been married in the Temple.

After Borga and Ethel visited with their relatives for a few days, they decided to take some short trips to points of interest in Cache Valley.

They had studied little in the field of geology, but from what Borga did know about it he imagined that there was much of interest in and about Cache Valley to anyone trained in this field. He wanted to learn more himself and he wanted Ethel to get some acquaintance with the subject.

During one of the short trips out of Logan into the mountains they ran into a camp of two men, with whom they stopped to chat, and found that they were geologists. They were delighted and, of course, asked lots of questions. They became so interested that they camped near them for three days.

Discussions with the geologist in their spare moments, together with some of their books which were examined briefly, put them in a position to be able to ask more intelligent questions. The geologists spent most of the last day they were with them answering questions and telling them more of the geological things of interest in and about the area.

Many of the past geological ages were represented by various structures in that area. Some of them, the geologists estimated ran back as much as four hundred million years. They were shown a great many samples of rock which had been collected. Also, quite a large number of fossils representing primitive life in some of the earlier geological ages. The valley came into its present formation through a series of structural adjustments or faults. These faults were brought about by a vertical cracking of the horizontal layer of rock formation.

The geologists traced some of these for them. They could point them out, both on the east and the west side of the valley and told them that the information available from their observations indicated that at an early period, formations were continuous. A violent upheaval caused a shift in these formations and a valley was formed between two remaining parts. They judged that the shift occurred in such a way that what remained was a sort of a bowl which now formed the rim of the valley. The smooth level floor of the valley resulted from lake and water action.

Due to the volcanic shift, the valley floor was lowered below the drainage outlet of the valley and it filled with water.

During one of the early glacial ages, the geologist estimated that the climate must have been much cooler than at present, and it had a greatly increased rainfall and probably much smaller evaporation. Many streams flowed at a much higher rate than they did at the present time. They thought that this natural phenomenon continued for many thousands of years and water accumulated in the great basin, which had no outlet to the ocean.

The lake that formed at that time was large and very deep. The geologists reasoned that the area had a probable maximum at its highest level of about nineteen thousand square miles, and a maximum depth of approximately one thousand feet.

This body of water was known to the geologists as Lake Bonneville. The lowest point of the lake was the bottom of the present great Salt Lake. During this Pleistocene age, which lasted for many thousands of years, the lake kept rising until it reached a maximum elevation of approximately 3,150 feet about sea level. During the climatic and structural changes taking place during succeeding geological ages, Lake Bonneville changed its level by several different discreet amounts. At each level, a bench was formed around the rim of the valley. These rims were evident to anyone observing the terrain in Cache Valley. As the level lowered, of course, the rivers cut through these benches, exposing the sides so that one could see the kind of material that was carried out before the level of the lake was changed.

Lake Bonneville existed during the glacial age, and the geologists pointed out several areas where glaciers had existed. They called attention to some of the indications left by the glaciers, the outflow from which, with the melting of the ice, increased the water supply of the lake tremendously.

Another thing of interest about Cache Valley was that its name was derived from the fact that the first white men entering the Valley were trappers and traders from the Hudson Bay and Northwest Fur Companies, and the Rocky Mountain Fur

Company. The representatives of the Rocky Mountain Fur Company were probably the first white men to enter Cache Valley, and they did this approximately one hundred years prior to the arrival of the Mormons.

The name Cache was given to the valley because that was where they cached their furs. Jim Bridger, as a young man, was with one of the early groups of trappers and, of course, became well known in the West in later years.

When they were alone after their visits with the geologists, it was clear that Ethel was disturbed to some extent by what she had heard. She commented: "The geological information does not seem to agree with the story in the Bible regarding the creation of the earth."

Borga agreed and mentioned, "The Bible presents this information as a revelation without substantiating facts. In geology, observations are made which appear to be facts, and the geologists try to interpret them without reference to any revelation as recorded in the Bible. The geologists develop their own hypothesis on the basis of the evidence which they find in nature. There may never be agreement in the two points of view."

Some of the Indians resorted to a considerable amount of stealing of livestock. Another difficulty that the Mormons were having in that area was an economic one. In order to pacify the Indians, they had to give them a certain amount of provisions. This taxed the Mormons since they had little to spare. But Brigham Young had advised them strongly that is was cheaper to feed the Indians than it was to fight them.

Because of their absence from Utah for several years Borga and Ethel's curiosity was particularly stimulated in the areas of economic and social development in the communities. Practically all the social activities of the towns took place at the meeting house, where they held church services. Socials were held in addition to religious services, and there was much visiting among the members. Much attention was given to cultural activities—music, public speaking, and singing. Education was given special emphasis.

Most of the economic life of the community was centered around the bishop's storehouse. Little money was available, and people exchanged their goods by barter. The prices for the various items were set at the bishop's storehouse, where storage was provided for butter, eggs, all sorts of farm produce. Feeding areas for livestock were provided. The tithing was paid into the bishop's storehouse, and all work being done for the church was paid for by giving the workmen credit so that they could buy anything which was available.

The bishop's storehouse, as it was usually called, was both the bank and the marketplace. It regulated the prices of commodities, including labor. It extended credit and served as a banking function. Facilities were available to handle important community investment projects.

Borga and Ethel went down several days to watch what was going on and were interested to find that a number of visitors had come in from the surrounding country and were camped in the area.

They also found that some poor people, who were unable to provide for themselves, were given relief in the form of credit for which they could buy what they needed. Brigham Young had set up these tithing houses, or bishop's storehouses, as stations for the mail service in the Mormon communities. The individual, carrying the mail, was paid in credit for his services, for which he could purchase such items as flour, eggs, wheat, and other produce.

Other things of interest to them during their stay in Logan was that it was noticeable that the Mormons were beginning to experience political difficulties similar to that which they experienced in the East. They nearly always voted as a block. It always gave them power, and this was, of course, antagonistic to the anti-Mormons.

One of the difficulties which was rapidly coming to the forefront was an anti-polygamy crusade. The law forbidding polygamy had only recently been passed. There was a strong political movement by the non-Mormons to have the law enforced, and once more a great amount of interference by anti-Mormons was experienced in the Mormon community.

The anti-Mormon activity was not as intense at Logan as it was at Salt Lake City. There were a number of polygamist families in the area. Borga and Ethel estimated about seven per cent of the married men had more than one wife.

Because of the difficulty that these men were experiencing, some of them had split their families up and sent one wife and family to Canada or to Mexico, while one family remained in the Utah area. But Borga's father was resisting such an action as long as possible.

32

Back in Washington, Borga tackled his legal work with his usual zeal. This was done at the office, but he acquired an extensive library on religions of the world, which he kept at his home. Most of the work on the verisimilitude of religions, which he decided to entitle *Essence of Desire*, was done there. He worked as if his life was at stake.

Ethel studied their literature almost as extensively as did Borga. They had many interesting discussions on the subject. All of the first pencil draft of the manuscript was made at home, a chapter at a time, and was then taken to the office for the final draft. Ethel did not see any of the final drafts until it was finished, about eighteen months after they returned to Washington. He brought the completed manuscript home one night just as he was leaving on a trip for a few days.

"I think it is in final form. Will you read it before I present it to a publisher?"

This she was eager to do. "I'm so proud of your efforts, Borga. I know in general what is in here, but I'm largely ignorant as to the details, so I shall read it with pleasure and enthusiasm."

As soon as he left, she started to read and kept at it incessantly. She wanted to complete it before he returned. In a quick review, she noted that the order he had used in discussing the various religions put the chapter on Mormonism at the end, and that he had called it an indigenous religion of America. Both of these decisions seemed to her to be appropriate since most of the other Christian sects were imported from Europe.

She decided to read the treatments in the order in which he had arranged them. She was especially eager to get at the discussion of her own religion, but that was at the end and with some anxiety she could wait. She hoped that he would have some nice things to say about it but knowing his penchant for honesty she realized that he would present it as the facts indicated.

She had studied the literature in their library quite thoroughly and felt that she was in a reasonable favorable position to evaluate his treatment of the subjects. As she read each chapter, she found little with which to disagree.

That was the case until she arrived at the chapter on Mormonism. There she didn't like what she found. She thought he had done a disservice to his own religion. She was extremely distraught over what she found and tried to justify in her own mind the feeling she had.

The reading of the manuscript was just completed as Borga returned. The long kiss which she gave him, he noted, was accompanied by tearful, red eyes. She reluctantly answered his excited pleading as to the cause of her grief by exclaiming, "Oh, Borga! How could you do such a thing?" He pressed for meaning to her question, but when it did not come, he quickly thought it best to question her on her reaction to the manuscript in the early chapters where he knew that she could take a more objective view.

"Do you think that I have given an honest interpretation of the facts in the case of the Jewish theology?"

"Yes, I think that the treatment is fine in all chapters until you got to our own religion. What you have in that chapter will make so many people unhappy. People we love." She burst into tears again. "Why did you have to do it?"

He attempted to discuss it further by inquiring, "Did you find anything in that chapter that was not true, or that I have been dishonest about, or have distorted in any way?"

She continued to weep but did not answer. He tried to soothe her. "I look upon this manuscript," he said, "almost as much a result of your efforts as of my own, and I shall be eager to discuss any change with you."

Ethel had taken possession of Mormonism. It was hers. She was like a mother guarding her young. She would do battle with any intruder. She was not in a state to be rational at this point, so

Borga suggested that they delay any further discussion until sometime later.

After seeing how it made her feel, he gave much thought to the subject during the evening, and concluded that her happiness was much more important than the manuscript.

Next morning, as he was kissing her before leaving for work, he eased into the subject. "Darling, I have decided to let the manuscript *soak* for a while. Maybe I have been too close to it for too long. We shall discuss it no further."

Actually, he had decided to lock it up and let it die. Her warm kisses and affection led him to suspect that she was activated by a sense of deep reproach and, perhaps, injury.

She didn't say no, but she had some remorseful feelings that he intended to do no more with it. It was his way of letting it slip into the Never-Never Land. His putting their love above his ambition to make a contribution with the publication of his manuscript gave a slight boost to her ego, however.

During the next few months, he showed no indication of rancor or displeasure over the manuscript situation. There was no sign of his feeling a martyr nor of his expecting her to make any payment for any magnanimous attitude on his part. She did, however, notice that his eyes seemed more than usual to be attracted to other items than to her. There was a slight attitude, not of hostility, but of coolness and excessive interest in his business.

She began to give more time to introspection—an effort at objective assessment of her own actions—of the merits of *Essence of Desire*, and the contribution that it would make. Her distress may have perverted her imagination of its merits, and probably was prompted in part by anguish which she felt when she observed that he was resting less well at night. His sleep seemed to her much more disturbed than was normal for him. She was not aware that this conclusion on her part might be because she was not sleeping well herself and, therefore, was more perceptive of his behavior during his sleeping hours.

The manuscript had laid dormant for almost a year, during which time Borga had gone about his work with his usual buoyant and unfettered manner. The subject of the manuscript, if it came up at all, was always dropped by him in preference for other—what he made appear—were more interesting topics.

Her anxiety mounted until finally she resolved to do something about it. "The manuscript should be brought out of storage, and I shall do everything in my power to get the book published," she kept thinking.

When he came home one night, she approached the subject with some apprehension because of his expressed desire not to discuss the subject. He listened to her plea: "I have completely changed my mind and now feel that my attitude before was not justified. After much thought, I have concluded that the manuscript must be published."

"Ethel, dear, I don't think that we should discuss that subject anymore, so please let's drop it right now." He even showed a spurt of anger, which was a rare thing for him to do, but to no avail. Ethel was adamant. His anger neither injured her feelings nor irked her but gave her assurance that he suffered and would consider himself unworthy if he neglected to present his work for publication. She concluded that if he did not, he would just be another of the multitude of men who had yielded their honor and their just place in society for attractive, lovely wives' tears and caresses and a quiet home life. His adroitness at covering the pain only made her love him more.

As the manuscript was being revised, her thoughts were fixed on her husband. Her love for him mounted, but she was ever conscious that she was responsible for the most tormenting influence that had entered her husband's life. Remorsefulness caused her hours of tearful depression.

One evening, when Borga came home, he remarked, "Ethel, dear, I have been thinking over the possibility that if the manuscript is ever published, the impact that it may have on public opinion in some quarters may have an effect on our legal business."

"I suppose that is possible, Borga. Do any members of the firm know the nature of the book?"

"No. I'm wondering whether it might be a good thing to invite them to read it and then get their opinion."

"I think that would be desirable. Wouldn't it also be worthwhile to invite them to have a general discussion of the manuscript after they have read it?"

"I agree, and I shall start the ball a-rolling in the morning."

Six weeks later, after the other members of the firm and their wives had completed reading the manuscript, Borga and Ethel invited them to their home for a discussion.

Borga announced, "We have invited you here tonight for several reasons. The first is that we enjoy your company. The second is that Ethel and I would appreciate receiving your evaluation of the manuscript. We would appreciate getting your frank criticism. It may save us some unfavorable criticism, if it is ever published; and third, I don't want it to bring unfavorable reactions on our legal firm.

"I suggest that first we discuss the merits of the manuscript and follow that with any thoughts as to its effect on our legal firm. Since you read it first, Ansel, I think it would be helpful if you would give us a thumbnail review of the subject matter covered in the manuscript." He turned to Ansel McCormick.

"Your manuscript was somewhat startling to me since I had not given much thought to such subjects. I was impressed with the way in which you treated the complex maze of ideas in each of the various mythologies and religions you covered. You have attempted rather successfully, it seems to me, to find the basic verifiable facts upon which each religion is built."

Borga then turned to Ben Cohen. "Do you have any ideas that you would like to add at this point, Ben?"

"I was impressed," said Ben, "with the small number of basic facts which can or have been verified, upon which the fantastic theological and religious mental edifices have been constructed by the fertile imaginations of men. From your discussions, I conclude that the verisimilitude of religions is not in the main based on verifiable facts but rather on an appeal to the emotions. The imaginary edifice constructed for the various religions gives them an imaginary verisimilitude which is satisfying to the members. It is what they want."

"Does that mean that they are trying to lift themselves by their bootstraps?" asked Ansel.

"That is about what it means," answered Ben.

Borga faced George Bunder. "George, you have been rather quiet so far. What are your thoughts?"

"It seemed to me to say that all religions are largely based on imagination. They are based on faith, which as the Apostle Paul said, in part, is 'the substance of things hoped for,' and which you have paraphrased in your titled as *Essence of Desire*."

"And it raised the question as to whether all the Gods, or their equivalents, of the various religions are imaginary."

Ethel said, "I would like to find out what some of the girls think."

Mrs. Bunder responded, "If our religions are based largely on imagination, and the members rely on the verisimilitude which it supplies, does our religion really do us any good?"

"I think it does," replied Mrs. McCormick. "It furnishes a pattern or model from which we can teach our children."

"I wonder about that," commented Mrs. Cohen. "Might we not be better off if we started teaching our children only the facts which can be verified in a natural way. The stimulation and beauty supplied by the facts of nature might be a better patten or model to follow than our religions. Might we not think of that as a more rational basis for a religion with more potential than those to which we owe allegiance now?"

Mrs. Bunder asked, "Borga, you have spent much time, and given much thought to the various religions. You indicate that each religion tends to have a particular concept of God or His equivalent, and even within each religion each thoughtful individual tends to have his own variation of that concept; and even most individuals change their concept of God as they mature. After all of your studies, do you believe that there is a God?"

"As pointed out in the manuscript," said Borga, "my purpose has not been to prove or support any concept. I have tried to present the information as objectively as possible. I can find no verifiable evidence that God exists. Neither can I find any evidence that He does not exist. It seems to me that it would be just as foolish to say that God does not exist as it is to say adamantly that He does exist."

Mrs. Cohen asked, "What about our concepts of heaven and hell?"

"I could find no evidence in any of your discussions of the various religions that an individual has a life before this one or a life after this one," commented Ansel.

"That is correct, except I tried to point out in the last chapter we all recognize that each living individual acts somewhat as the narrow neck of a funnel through which the genes of our multi-tudinous ancestors pass on to our multitudinous descendants, if we have any. It is interesting to recognize that each individual, as he passes through this funnel, carried some of the genes that were living in his multitudinous ancestors, and some of which may continue to be living in his many descendants, if he has such. This could be considered 'the funnel of life.' In this natural way we might think of an individual as having a life before this one and life after this one; albeit they would seem to be very diffuse existences."

Mrs. McCormick said, "We are told by the Scriptures that God made man. I gather that you could find no evidence, except the Scriptures, that this is so."

"In my treatment I did not regard reports of supernatural events as verifiable evidence. I regarded the scriptures as historical accounts. We have to recognize that they have been translated, and in some cases several times, so that some of the accounts have to be interpreted as 'somebody said that somebody said that somebody said that God said.' This leaves us with many un-answered questions."

"Ben, you seem to have something on your mind," Borga noted.

"Yes, I have. Assuming that your manuscript presents a fair picture of the situation, and I believe that it does, we must conclude that the verisimilitude which various people in each religion accept, is derived almost exclusively from imaginary bases. Since our ethics and morals are almost inextricably tied in with our religious teachings, I'm wondering what would happen to them if these ideas, so clearly presented in your manuscript, are recognized."

"I believe," said Ansel, "that we don't need to worry too much about that because only a very few people, even after reading the manuscript, will recognize the validity of its information. Most people will go right on being happy with their imaginary verisimilitude. Fortunately, a few people will gradually begin to think about the more valid basis for ethics and morals, as a result of such studies as Borga has made."

"Next, I would like to get your opinion as to whether this manuscript, if published, will react unfavorably in any way on our firm."

Ben answered. "I see no way in which this could cause un-favorable criticism of our firm. The closest that this might occur is that, to anyone who reads it carefully, questions may arise as to the validity of some of our rituals used in the public swearing-in of officials and in some of our national songs and pledges. But I do not regard this as serious."

"I agree," said Ansel. "Perhaps some rational question on such items might be in order."

Borga was about to close the discussion, but he noticed that Mrs. Bunder wanted to speak.

"I'm afraid that I'm one of those on whom this manuscript and our discussion tonight has had a marked effect. I doubt if I shall ever be able to give my children as convincing lessons in their religion as I could have done before reading the book. For instance, when I talk to my children about heaven, angels and God, I will-consciously or not-have a tendency to hedge on the ideas which I try to convey to them about religion. As I teach religious principles to my children in the future, I am afraid that I shall be a little less definite than I have been before tonight. I don't know whether this is good or bad, but I think it is a fact."

33

Considerable revision took placed on the book. Ethel was anxious to give her advice and help during the revision and she had complied with that desire. It was completed and accepted for publication.

A few days later she received a letter from her parents. They had been "called" to take up the task as Mormon missionaries in the eastern states. They would arrive in Washington in about one month.

Borga's treatment of Mormon theology—and, perhaps, much of that of other religions—would be completely unacceptable to her father. When the book was published, it would be considered by him a vital blow to their missionary work. Her anxiety depressed her and took more of her time. She became pale and weak. Borga insisted that she go to see a doctor. The medication which the doctor prescribed proved ineffective.

She brooded over her disappointment in life when she recalled the struggle she had made to join the Mormon church, and the testimony she had borne in fast meetings many times, in which she prayed for three things: the ability to marry the man of her choice; the ability to be a good mother to their children; and the ability to go through the Mormon Temple and be sealed to her husband and family for life and eternity.

She pondered the results. The first part of her prayer had been satisfied. She had married the man of her choice, but against her father's wishes. She felt that she had been unjust to her husband in that she had caused him deep grief regarding the manuscript.

She had hoped for children, but she had been unable to have any. And, of course, going through the Mormon Temple to be sealed to her husband was out of the question since Borga, even if he wished to go, could not get a recommendation from his bishop.

Borga's excitement at the completion of his manuscript, at her insistence, put him in a more buoyant mood than he had been in for some time. If it were not for her seemingly failing health, he felt that she could really enjoy life.

He hoped that the arrival of her parents would help to make her feel better. The day they were to arrive he left work and went home to get Ethel, so that they could go to the railroad station where her folks were to arrive.

He entered his home and not finding her ready went upstairs to her bedroom. To his horror, she was on the bed, unconscious. He immediately called the neighbors who went for the doctor. When the doctor arrived, he told Borga that his wife was dead. On the table was an empty bottle which had contained pills. The doctor had prescribed that she should use them sparingly, and they should have lasted her for a month.

The End

About the Author

Niels Edlef Edlefsen was born in Logan, Utah, in 1893. He obtained his B.S. degree from Utah State University in 1916 and his Master's and Doctor's degrees in Physics from the University of California at Berkeley in 1923 and 1930. "Ed" worked with E.O. Lawrence and J.R. Oppenheimer at Berkeley on the photoionization of metallic vapors and in the develop-ment of high-speed protons. He also constructed the first cyclotron and demonstrated its use. Ed held positions with the faculties of Utah State University, the University of California at Davis and at Gadja Mada University in Jogiakarta, Indonesia. He also served with distinction in the US Army during WW1 and WW2. This work of fiction was a "retirement project" prior to his passing in Davis, CA in 1970.